C000089301

Published in Great Britain by

L.R. Price Publications Ltd., 2022.
27 Old Gloucester Street,
London,
WC1N 3AX
www.lrpricepublications.com

Cover artwork by by Aneesa Cassimjee.
Aneesa Casimjee, Copyright 2022

Used under exclusive and unlimited licence by

L.R. Price Publications Ltd.

ISBN-13: 9781915330079

THE BOG

BOGLUNS OF

BALLINALEE

John Hughes

KELLERBEG BOG

Have you ever strolled down a quiet country lane around dusk on a balmy summer's evening just as the sun is starting to slide behind a flower-laden hill? Then heard rustling in a ditch alongside where you are walking; even seen a flash of colour, the colour being too brief or quick to realise what it is? You may have been close to a boglun.

These creatures move very quickly, skipping over marshy surfaces with large, flat, kipper feet designed to run on wet ground. Their skin is pale and dappled and sometimes dark, depending on the time of year. They have protruding teeth to gnaw carrots and bog grasses and also the incredible capability to change colour, similar to a chameleon; blending into their surroundings if startled or spotted. The only thing that does not change colour is their hair. They also emit a horrible smell if cornered, just like skunks.

Bogluns have short, stubby noses and big eyes for night vision. Their ears are so large and pointy that they can hear even a leaf or branch rustle. Their fingers are long and spindly for picking fruit and turf bracken, as this is their favourite food.

Having explained what these creatures look like, I am going to tell you a story about a boglun family that lived near our farm, close to the local bog of Kellerbeg.

The head of our boglun family is Dada Muklefinn, his wife and the mother is Mammy, the mischievous son is Murf and the daughter is Twiggle. The Muklefinns have lived for many generations on the boglands with their kinfolk back through time. But with modern farming, machinery and roads, their lands are fast diminishing, causing the clans to move many times throughout history.

The boglun lord is named Grizzle the Iron Jaw due to his large, poisonous, black teeth and being **three times** the size of a normal boglun. He is very rarely seen and lives in an underground kingdom from where he rules the creatures of his domain. Folklore tells us that he can make you fall asleep if you stare into his big cat-like eyes, and no one dares to make Grizzle angry. Bogluns only need to see him if they are sick or need a spell or potion. He never goes into the sunlight, has dark, bumpy skin like a frog and is as fat as a football.

His queen, the Princess Fannah, is from a fairy dynasty many years past and is daughter to the High Elfin Lord Nemus of the Northwind. It was said throughout history that Princess Fannah had been captured by humans and never seen since. Lord Grizzle never got over or believed it and has disliked humans since she vanished. Broken-hearted, he longs to find news of her and hides away in his underground lair, never going into daylight. Every day he sends his weasel army out to search for her, travelling many miles across waterways and woodlands in their quest. The large boglun sheds many tears each day, hoping she might return to mend his broken heart, but she is now becoming a distant memory as the long days pass.

Grizzle used to be a tall, fine creature with silk-like skin and a beautiful head of shiny, orange hair and all bogluns used to greatly admire him. Now, however, he is hideous and old and his eyes are black and piercing. He collects his tears in old bottles that have been scavenged from the humans, which are then mixed with wasp spit and spun into a thread-type material by large spiders, which resembles a silver-like candyfloss called spiddywizzle.

This magic wizzle is only given to the bog-land creatures if they are sick or injured; it can also freeze anything if thrown at you, so when mixed together this magical potion will cure any illness you may have. However, there is a price to pay for spiddywizzle. Each year the boglun clans collect what they call dazzle, which is anything that shines or glitters. Gold is the favourite but rarely found.

Each year at the harvest's end when the autumn leaves start to fall, bogluns make the journey by river to Grizzle's lair to give offerings for his protection and spiddywizzle. The bogluns then dance and sing in large circles for a good winter and spring the following year, creating fairy rings and flattening the grass around them as they celebrate.

No one knows what Grizzle does with all the dazzle. Some say he adorns the walls of his underground kingdom with bottle tops and anything that glitters; some say he saves it for his beloved Princess Fannah so that one day she will return.

The lair to Grizzle's domain is guarded night and day by river weasels. These creatures are not very friendly and there are many of them. The head weasel is named Maldruff and he would not hesitate to attack you to protect the high boglun's lair. They give allegiance to Lord Majestic Grizzle in return for the wizzle that he places at the cave entrance when it is needed. The weasels constantly patrol the flowing waterways and bogs, in case of attack on his domain to steal his treasure.

On a beautiful summer morning, as the breeze fluttered through the bog grass and the sun climbed high into the sky, Dada woke Murf and Twiggle early from their comfy beds of fern wands and goose feathers, deep within the sturdy oak tree on the edge of the bog. The comfy home went deep under the old tree and had many rooms, all kept tidy by Mammy and Twiggle. Bogluns are terrible collectors of junk and trinkets and use all manner of things to make their homes nice.

Their prized possession is eggshells, which are used as water containers, buckets or even crash helmets... which was how Murf would often use them.

After breakfast, the trio were getting ready to go foraging for large mushrooms and sitting in a nearby oak tree was Cornelius the crow - Corny to his friends. Corny is a sort of postman, messenger and watchman combined. He takes messages and letters to the surrounding boglun clans and also warns them if anything dangerous is about such as barkies (dogs), fluffers (foxes) or stripeys (badgers). All of these animals are dangerous to bogluns, as they can get eaten if they don't have their wits about them.

During the summer months, the field mushrooms pop up at dawn and glisten in the dewy morning sun, only to disappear by midday. No one knows where they go, but they are gone. Murf's sleepy head looked up from his breakfast of gooseberry porridge and announced to his sister, 'I tink dem mishrooms are munched by da Monsta Mishroom Muncher.'

'Ah Murf, ye is full of stories. Dere's no such thing as a Mishroom Muncher,' replied Twiggle.

'Stop your cackle, Murf! Ye will scare your sister,' said Dada. 'Get your toggles (clothes) on. We're off for mishrooms for Mammy's larder.'

Bogluns wear simple clothes that resemble dungarees. They are woven from wool gathered from barbed wire fences where the sheep scratch and leave loose fleece. When all stitched together with ivy vine thread, they look very smart.

Collecting mushrooms sounds a simple enough task, but when you are twelve inches tall and the grass comes up to your chin, it is not so easy to pick a mushroom that is as big as a dustbin lid to a boglun.

'One each is all we can roll back home,' said Dada to Murf and Twiggle. 'And watch out for barkies.'

The local farmyard barkie is called Buddy and he loves to chase bogluns but never catches any because he is now too old to go running around.

'Don't worry, Dada, I will,' replied Murf. 'Da barkies are still sleeping and nowhere near da mishrooms.'

Bogluns have a very funny voice, which is very high-pitched, although you can still understand them when they speak. Their language is called Boglish and has been passed down over generations from listening to humans.

Dada brought his crubeknocker and put it in his rucksack. A crubeknocker is a very sharp type of axe made from stone on one end, a handle made from old tree branches and a knob on the other end for bonking barkies or fluffers on the nose if they get too close. A crubeknocker is also needed to chop mushroom stems, so the bogluns can roll them home before Buddy the barkie or the humans wake up.

'If dat silly barkie comes anywhere near me, I'm gonna parp him,' Murf proudly exclaimed. Parping is a boglun expression to make a foul smell like a skunk before running away across the wet bogs, a place Buddy would not be keen to go, or for that matter get parped at. Buddy had a score to settle with Murf, as he had previously been parped when he'd caught him in the farm's henhouse collecting feathers from the baggaas (chickens in Boglish). There had been a big hoo-ha that day when all the hens fled from their roosts with the pong and poor Buddy had to stick his nose in the chickens' water trough to escape the smell.

Dada had warned Murf repeatedly about snooping around the humans' farmstead, as they might see or catch him or, even worse,

Buddy could eat him! Like any naughty boy, he always ignored his mother's and father's warnings, and regularly wandered around Farmer McNally's land looking for trinkets or shiny things, from bottle tops to bits of mirror. If it glittered, Murf would collect it.

Little did he realise that his next visit may be his last as Farmer McNally now had a new barkie called Golly. Buddy was getting old and needed a young, faster dog to help him round up the sheep each evening. Murf was due to find out very soon just how fast and nasty the new barkie would be when chasing a boglun.

Mammy and Twiggle were busy back at their oak tree house, hastily sweeping up dust and old acorn shells that Murf had been eating the night before and had stuffed under his bed.

'I am goin to be talkin to dat boy. His bedroom's a disgrace to the land of Ballinalee,' Mammy exclaimed.

Twiggle had heard it all before. 'Ah Mammy, you'll just be telling him he is naughty and he will not be takin heed of ye.'

'Not if I tell Dada,' replied Mammy. 'He will be put at collectin da marsh grass down at da well to make new comfy beds.'

Dada then shouted out, 'Where is dat little gabblegob? I've not laid eyes on him since stacking da mishrooms this morning.'

'You'd need eyes on stalks to be seeing him,' replied Twiggle.

Further down the field, the long, swaying wheat and barley bobbed and glistened in the morning sun and buttercups turned their faces to the warmth of the day. Suddenly, a flash of orange darted in and out of the swaying stems and the grass rustled. It was Murf skipping through the field at a furious pace with his long legs jumping just like a frog. He stopped dead in his tracks and scooted up a barley stem and froze. His skin changed colour to match the long shards of barley around him.

Murf could hear rustling in the distance, gradually increasing to thumping and crunching. He looked down and spied Gribbo the bullfrog. 'Oh Gribbo, ye had me well-startled. I was thinking ye was a barkie.'

Grunt, wheeze and grunt came from the elderly frog. 'Oh Murf,' exclaimed Gribbo, 'I am making a noise like a groundstripper.' (A groundstripper is a combine harvester or tractor). 'You had best be leaving this field quick as the humans are bringing one into the meadow. I have seen them feeding it with wiffy juice (petrol). You must know when it drinks wiffy it roars and smoke comes from its tail, and it gets really angry eating all the field, chopping and munching.'

'Ah, be calm,' replied Murf. 'Hop on my back and I will take ye to da riverbank.' Gribbo reluctantly agreed and jumped on Murf's back. The great weight made him wheeze but off Murf stumbled through the long, swaying bog grass with Gribbo hanging on for dear life.

'Will you slow up, Murf?' Gribbo moaned. 'I'm getting all bamjangled with your swinging.'

'Ah Gribbo, I could be goin faster,' mumbled Murf. 'But ye must of bin atein stones. Ye are such a lump!'

'Put me to the ground immediately!' Gribbo demanded of Murf. 'I am not taking insults from you, you spindly little bogtrotter. Dada will hear of your rudeness to the senior frog of this townland. I'm the finest frog that ever hopped these fields!'

'Ha-ha,' laughed Murf. 'Dada is busy and won't be takin heed of ye,' replied Murf.

'Huh,' Gribbo grumbled and he hopped away, very disgruntled.

Murf meets Golly

Now, in Murf's mind, a visit up and around the McNally farm could be fruitful and worthwhile on this sunny morning. He might come across eggshells or even dazzle. Murf slid around the back of McNally's rickety, old henhouse with his little straw sack slung across his shoulder. He peered through a broken crack in the splintery old boards. Slowly, the crafty boglun popped his orange mop of hair inside the darkness of the henhouse and all was quiet. The baggaas were out in the yard, pecking corn left down for them by Farmer McNally.

Murf's eyes widened to saucer-like proportions as he suddenly spied three broken eggshells. 'Wow!' he squeaked as he shuffled along the straw-filled shelves.

Just as he was within touching distance, Murf's long, feathery fingers reached out to grab his prize but echoing from the shadows, a terrible rumble started and the ground shook intensely. Out of the gloomy darkness, a large, dark object charged across the straw-covered floor with sharp teeth glinting like razor blades.

Murf froze like a statue, not knowing whether to run, scream or cry. He instinctively changed colour blending into his surroundings of straw and was now so scared he released an awful parp into the henhouse.

Oh jeez! Murf thought to himself. Wot is dat hairy ting below?

It was the new farm dog, Golly, teeth bared with his shaggy black fur standing on end. Suddenly, Golly got a whiff of an awful smell and looked around but could not see anything in the dim light of the henhouse, only shadows. The smell increased and Golly, nearly overcome by the stink, then ran out of the henhouse huffing and puffing to clear his nose of the awful smell. Instantly, Murf swung himself upside down, grabbing the shed's rafters with his long fingers and flipping himself up outside and onto the roof. He changed colour again to match the dull-grey tin surface and stayed motionless until the large, black barkie walked away back to his kennel.

It was a close shave for Murf and one not to experience again. But being Murf, he still wanted the eggshells so, slowly, he swung silently back into the hens' roost again and collected up the shells. He neatly stacked them into each other and carefully placed them into his sack. Murf stared at the last cracked shell and spun it around in his spindly fingers. Now dat wud make a fine crash hat in case da barkie returns he thought, and promptly stuck it on his head. He squeezed his orange hair out each side and twisted and turned it until his new hat was quite comfy.

Now the little boglun was convinced he was ready for battle with anyone and let out little giggles as he adjusted his new crown. His silly grin and front teeth were protruding just like a rabbit's. Oh, what a sight he was. What would Dada, Mammy or Twiggle think if they saw the silly boglun boy?

Murf scurried along the henhouse roof, looking left and right and imagining he was a soldier on a secret mission to outwit the barkies. He hopped like a toad from the henhouse on to the farmhouse roof, dodging and darting between the chimney stacks across the slippery black slates until he was at the end of the building. Looking around, he slid down the drainpipe onto the window ledge of an upstairs bedroom and very cautiously peered around the curtain. His helmet slowly slid off due to it being very slimy when he stuck it on his head.

Again, he wiggled and waggled the eggshell back into position with a big, silly grin at his sense of achievement so far. Suddenly, Murf's gaze spotted a wonder of all wonders to a boglun. 'Oh my goggly gosh,' he exclaimed to himself. There inside the window, a beautiful, gold pendant hung on the arm of a dressing table mirror. This was a wonder to the little boglun. The sun reflected off the beautiful jewel and blue and red stones glittered like a hundred mirrors in the dappled light, as it reflected onto the bedroom walls.

It was the bedroom of Farmer McNally's daughter Nellie who was ten years old. Oh, to a boglun's eyes it was treasure beyond his wildest dreams. It was so beautiful that it would make him the finest, the cleverest, the most brilliant and famous boglun ever, ever in the whole of the land! What a hero he would be and he imagined the praise from Grizzle for finding such dazzle as this. Murf was now in dream world. His eggshell crash hat was now a crown of kings. His spidery legs swung to and fro over the window ledge as his big, flat feet swayed in the wind. Murf had made the big time, but now, if he could just get the shiny jewel.

Bogluns do not understand you cannot steal or take other people's property. To them, you can have anything if you can lift and carry it.

Murf took a deep breath and then swung in behind the curtain through the open window. His little heart pounded in his chest as he peered at the sparkly jewel. It was clearly in sight and nearly in his grasp. Murf slid down the curtains and scooted under the little single bed in Nellie's room. Pushing smelly socks and teddy bears to one side, he peered out from between the mountain of old rubbish. Suddenly, a noise came from the hallway. Startled, Murf froze, turning teddy-bear brown to blend in with his surroundings. Nellie suddenly re-entered her bedroom after forgetting to close her window. Slam! Down it crashed, now trapping him under her bed.

Murf dared not scoot out of the room into the hallway, as this was a strange and alien place to him. What dangers might be beyond that door? So he remained still and quiet as Nellie turned around and left, shutting the door firmly behind her. Now, little Murf was really trapped.

All afternoon, he climbed up and down the curtains, pulling and pushing at the window trying to release it, but it would not budge. It was now getting late. The evening sun went down and a chill filled the air. Oh, goggly, thought Murf. I'm really stuffed now. So, very scared, he hid in between the old socks and teddies.

Back at home, the family were becoming increasingly concerned about Murf as he had not been seen since morning. Dada went off searching the lower meadows while Mammy and Twiggle searched down at the creek as he often played around there, but nothing. The sound of grass crickets and the trickle of water filled the evening air and an eerie silence fell upon the homestead.

Bogluns have a sound they emit, like the sound of a rattle, to find each other if in long grass or meadows. It's called cackling. They also jump up into the air so their orange hair can be seen by other bogluns. Mammy and Twiggle jumped and cackled for ages but still no Murf. Meanwhile, Dada went to see wise old Gribbo near the river and explained that Murf had not been seen all day. Everyone was out looking and were now very concerned and worried.

Gribbo lifted his green eyebrow. 'He's a naughty little wagglegob,' he remarked. 'He has insulted the finest frog in Ballinalee today by implying my proportions were large! Why don't you ask Cornelius to fly around and see if he can spot the silly wagglegob anywhere?' said Gribbo.

'That's a great idea!' exclaimed Dada. 'I will ask Corny to have a flutter about.' By the time Dada got back home, Mammy and Twiggle had also returned. Mammy was sobbing and

Twiggle desperately tried to comfort her, but a big tear rolled down her cheek as they bogglehugged. It was too dark for Corny to fly and look for Murf now. He would not be able to see anything in the darkness. He would have to wait 'til daylight, and they would need to worry all night as to their beloved Murf's fate.

As dawn broke the next morning, Cornelius awoke from his nest in the big oak tree. He stretched and flapped his large, black silky wings towards the morning sun. Corny knew he was going to have a busy day, so he cleaned and pruned his feathers to make them sleek and smart for his morning flight. Dada had already been pacing up and down beneath since daybreak, scratching his big, orange beard and waiting for the crow to wake.

'I am here, Dada and ready to fly,' shouted Cornelius.

Dada looked up at the big bird. He was very worried about his son being missing since yesterday and he rubbed his orange, stubbly head in despair.

'Be you ready fine, Corny, to seek my Murf?' cried out Dada. 'How far can your wings be takin ye?'

Corny shook his feathery head and replied, 'I will fly to the kingdom's edge, Dada, every day until I find him.' With that, off into the morning breeze he flew. Corny knew it was going to be hard as bogluns hide and also change colour, so all he could do was try.

Cornelius soared high above the treetops, swooping in and out over the meadows, along the riverbank and down around the chocolate-coloured peatland of Kellerbeg bog, but there was no sign of Murf. After an hour or so, Corny was getting tired and needed a quick rest in a tree to think of a plan to cover as much area as possible.

Little did anyone know that Murf had spent the night under Smelly Nellie's bed with her on top snoring. The little boglun was now getting very weak and lack of food and sleep had made him slow and sluggish. He could not change colour or parp anymore either. Nellie arose and threw back her bedclothes and with a big yawn, she stretched her arms into the air. She then felt under her bed for her frog-shaped slippers, narrowly missing Murf as her hand rooted about in the rubbish. Nellie stuffed her feet into the green slippers and shuffled over to the window and opened it.

This was Murf's chance to escape.

As Nellie turned towards the door, Murf shot out from under the bed and feverishly grasped the curtains to climb to freedom but was too weak. However hard he tried to climb, his little arms felt like lead and he slid to the floor.

Nellie, hearing the scrambling, turned around and spotted the boglun. She rushed over with a waste-paper basket and promptly plonked it over him.

'Ha-ha. I have caught a fairy,' Nellie cried. She ran into another room and returned with a rusty, old birdcage that she'd used to keep budgies in. She quickly scooped Murf up and deposited him in the cage, then promptly closed its door. Murf lay motionless in the dirty cage not able to stand nor cry out, so hungry and exhausted he slowly drifted into sleep.

Nellie was a cruel child and not wanting to let her parents know what she had, she tied a string around the top of the cage and hung it out of her bedroom window with a bowl of water and bread thrown in. Bogluns do not eat bread and Murf was too weak to drink, so he just lay beside the water bowl.

Hours passed as the morning sun became very strong, beating down on the helpless boglun wearing his eggshell helmet. The crash hat managed to keep the sun off his head at least. In the meantime, Corny had flown many miles and now was also exhausted but could not bear to return with no sighting or hope of finding Murf alive.

Corny gave one last thrust and swooped from the clouds down over the McNally's farmstead.

'Nothing! Nothing!' exclaimed Corny to himself as he glided into the north wind. Just then, a glint of orange caught his bird's sharp eye. He turned, dropping lower and swooped down over the farm, finally landing on the gutter of the house. From there, he could see the birdcage propped up and hanging on a string from the bedroom window. It was rattling and clanking up against the pebble wall in the morning breeze. At first, the crow thought it was a poor bird trapped in that awful prison, but then he noticed the eggshell and Murf's orange hair sticking out either side.

'By all the acorns!' Corny exclaimed. 'It's- it's Murf. It's Murf.'

The Rescue

Cornelius had found poor Murf but didn't know if he was alive or badly injured. His heart fluttered with anguish as he swooped down to get a closer look. The large bird landed on the window ledge, constantly looking all around in case the human child returned or the farm dogs spotted him. He gently tapped the cage with his large, yellow beak, but there was no response from Murf. He then ran it across the rusty bars with a clack, clack, clack, but still the little boglun did not stir. This was very serious and Corny feared for Murf's life. What was he going to tell Dada, Mammy and Twiggle? Corny squawked and again rattled the cage.

Slowly, one of Murf's big, flat feet twitched. 'Murf. Murf,' Corny squawked. 'It's me.' He rattled the bars a second time. Suddenly the little eggshell hat moved and a pair of bleary eyes squinted from under the helmet as it glinted in the morning sun.

'Oh Corny, is dat ye?' little Murf squeaked out.

'Yes, it's me,' replied Corny. 'What has happened to you?'

Murf explained in his high-pitched, weak voice about his antics and how Nellie had captured him; and now he was trapped in the cage.

'The problem is,' Corny exclaimed, 'how can I release you from here? The bars are metal and my beak cannot force the cage open. If I bite on the string, the cage will fall to the ground and you will be killed. Oh Murf, what is to be done, you silly boglun?' said the crow. 'You should never have gone into a human's house.' Corny looked in the window and saw that Smelly had gone down to breakfast, so at least they had a little time to try and effect a rescue.

Crows are very clever birds and Corny was the most intelligent when it came to solving problems. Just as he was thinking, the bedroom door flew open and Nellie bounced back in and started jumping on her bed. She had cornflakes stuck to her lips and milk still dribbling down her chin from her breakfast. Then remembering her fairy in the cage, she promptly opened the window to check on her little prisoner. With that, Corny took flight off the window ledge and circled above, frantically flapping to stay in one place. Nellie pulled up the cage and plonked it on her bed. She peered excitedly in between the bars to look at the little boglun, making plans for her fairy captive.

Nellie opened her school bag and pulled out a pencil. She then reached into the cage and poked Murf hard to see if he was still alive. The little boglun lay motionless, not stirring or moving as she repeatedly jabbed him.

'Wake up, Fairy,' Nellie cried, prodding him again and then sprinkling water on him from the dish to try and wake him. But still he lay silent. She reached into the cage and grabbed the little boglun in her hand. She squeezed him so hard he could hardly breathe before throwing his limp body on her pillow.

'I know,' Nellie said, 'maybe you want a cup of tea?' She ran over to her dollhouse and picked up a little, red, plastic cup. 'I am going downstairs to get you some. I won't be long.'

As Nellie left the room, Murf's big, blue saucer-like eyes opened and looked around for any movement. He then sat upright and jumped to his feet but started to suddenly sink into Nellie's dirty pillows. Murf was used to standing on surfaces that are spongy like the boggy ground at his home, but not like Smelly Nellie's pillow. Slowly, he stumbled along the bed to the edge of the blankets ready to jump over onto the window but he just had no strength left. He slumped onto one knee with his other leg dangling over the edge.

Corny, who was swooping around outside, on seeing the commotion flew in through the open window and landed beside the stricken boglun. 'Jump on my back quickly,' cried Corny.

Murf lifted his weary arm over Corny's large neck, then slid onto his silky back. The crow summoned up all his strength and with a powerful bound, leapt onto the window ledge with Murf hanging on for his life.

'Hang on tight. I am not able to fly with your weight and may crash to the ground. I will try and glide over to that pear tree in the field, so hang on.' Corny thrust his powerful legs off the ledge and with his large wings outstretched and into the morning breeze, away they both glided towards the tree. Bang and crash went the branches as they collided into the leafy foliage. They were free but not safe.

Corny steadied himself and slid the stricken boglun onto a sturdy branch. He weaved the twigs together with his beak to create a makeshift nest for poor Murf. 'I am going to get you some food and water and then fly back to Kellerbeg to tell your family you are safe. So, rest and don't you dare move!'

Murf raised his spindly arm and patted Corny on his feathery shoulder.

'Do you know the bedroom you were in?' exclaimed the crow. 'It was Smelly Nellie's. She's the cruellest child in the land. She pulls wings off butterflies and eats spiders too. What possessed you?'

Murf tried to explain that he'd seen the beautiful pendant and the temptation was just too much.

'Oh, you silly boglun,' said Corny. 'She leaves it there on purpose to attract silly magpies and fairies so she can lure them in and capture them. Lie quietly and rest. I am going for help.' Corny swooped off into the wind, slowly climbing upwards into the morning breeze and gliding down in search of food for Murf. He finally landed in a tree some miles away to see Maggie the magpie, his old friend. He informed her of Murf's plight and how he was lying helpless in the far-off pear tree.

Maggie agreed to fly over with acorn pie and pear juice to feed him. Corny could fly for Kellerbeg after he had rested and had some of Maggie's tasty pie.

After a short break, Corny adjusted his feathers. He had a full tummy and so had regained his strength for the long flight home to bring good news to the worried boglun family. He flew with all his strength, swooping and climbing high into the wind and his powerful wings flapping like the great bird he was.

Finally, after a tiring trip, he saw Kellerbeg in the distance below. He gently descended towards the oak tree home, spying Dada below sitting on a log with Lord Grizzle's head weasel Maldruff. Corny let out high-pitched squawks to signal his arrival.

Looking up, Dada jumped around with joy to see the mighty Cornelius returning.

As the big crow landed, Twiggle jumped on him, hugging the bird so hard his eyes started to pop out.

'Goggly, Twiggle,' Corny cried. 'You're squeezing my pie out of me.' He then exclaimed with joy, 'He's safe. Murf is safe. He is not out of trouble yet but I will explain later. Maggie Magpie is looking after him in the pear tree near McNally's farm.'

'Oh, what a place to be,' Dada exclaimed. 'I will marmalise him, da little scallywag. Wait 'til I get hold of himself.'

'Now, now,' Mammy sighed. 'Be grateful to the tree fairies that he is safe, that's all,' she said. So, with that good news they all bogglehugged with excitement, except for Maldruff who sat back stroking his long, slimy whiskers.

'So, my time has been wasted,' commented slimy Maldruff. 'I have been summoned to your bog-land for nothing. Dazzle will be due for my wasted journey.'

'Oh, your time is not wasted, Maldruff,' replied Corny. 'We need to hatch a plan to rescue Murf as he is weak and a long way from here.'

'What plan?' replied Maldruff. 'We don't waste our time with bold, little bogluns.'

'Please, help,' cried Mammy. 'We need help.'

Corny was a crafty crow and suggested a plan. 'We can build a boat of water reeds fastened together by ivy twine, which could be towed by the weasels to the bottom of McNally's farmland,' he suggested. 'Then on foot to Maggie Magpie's tree, hiding in the ditches to avoid barkies, then back to the river and home.'

Maldruff rolled his watery eyes. 'You will need a large dazzle for such a feat as this. And more weasels to tow the boat there and back,' replied Maldruff.

Dada then replied, 'Yes, oh yes, I will find dazzle for your weasels but, please, help.'

Within an hour, all the bogluns were out cutting bog reeds and ivy twine for the great construction. Mammy and Twiggle collected the twine, Dada was busy cutting reeds and Corny flew back and forth, collecting the boat parts required. Slowly, the vessel was completed and the bogluns fastened long ivy ropes for the weasels to pull through the water.

Finally, it was ready and looked very fine. Dada made seats for the family, using duck feathers and ferns on the floor, in case Murf was too ill to sit up.

Maldruff and his weasels dragged the little boat to the river and pushed it in. Bloosh! The rescue craft glided into the crystal-clear water and the ripples washed over Dada's big, flat feet.

Dada and Maldruff clambered onto the boat that was bobbing up and down on the edge of the riverbank but Twiggle and Mammy remained at home to prepare hot buttercup soup and acorn buns for everyone upon their return. Dada had mushroom pie and crab apple juice for the journey all packed into his straw sack for the trip, which was stored in the little boat under the seat.

As dusk fell, the sun started to disappear down behind the hill and a mist started to creep across the river. The group set off with the water weasels towing the little, green boat through the rushes and water grass. Many hours passed as the small vessel glided effortlessly through marshland. The fine dew descended upon Dada wrapped up in his fern blanket while Maldruff sat proudly at the bow of the craft. His eyes scanned the river, sniffing the night air as he tugged on the ivy reins to hurry the water weasels on through the night.

Many hours passed but finally they arrived. 'We are here,' Maldruff barked. 'Pull the boat into those reeds and tie it to that log,' he hissed at the other weasels.

Once secured, Dada and Maldruff jumped onto the riverbank and sat under the long grass, yawning and very tired. For the next few hours, they both slept wrapped under the blankets that Mammy had packed for them. The weasels, in the meantime, curled up on the riverbank for a nap too. As the sun started to rise above the trees, the dappled shadows bounced upon the marshy land through the drifting mist, and blue-tailed dragonflies started dancing upon the shimmering river as it flowed gently through the land. As the fog started to burn away in the morning light, Dada opened one eye from under a bushy eyebrow and stroked his big, orange beard. He stretched out his arms towards the morning sun as the weasels shook and preened their shiny, waterproof coats. Maldruff was snorting and grumbling as he normally did.

They covered the little boat in ferns and river grass to hide it from nosey animals and prying eyes, then set off through the long grass towards Maggie Magpie's tree to meet Corny, who was flying down that morning. Dada was now getting excited to see little Murf at last.

Dada plodded through the long, grassy banks of the river, with Maldruff and his weasel soldiers going ahead to ensure the coast was clear from barkies **and** stripeys.

These animals were always looking for a boglun to eat and as they climbed the grassy bank, they could see Cornelius circling in the morning air above the magpie's tree.

'We are nearly there,' cried Maldruff. 'I can see Corny.'

Dada stood bolt upright in the grass. His orange head poked above the swaying meadow grass.

'Keep your head down, you silly boglun,' cried Maldruff. 'We are close to the McNally's farm and the barkies may spot you.'

Dada ducked down excitedly. 'Sorry, Maldruff,' he said. 'Wees exciting on seeing Murf,' he exclaimed in his boglish voice.

As they approached the old pear tree, Maggie Magpie swooped down to the lower branches and welcomed the little rescue party. The soldier weasels darted in and out of the long grass, sniffing the air with their long, sharp noses. Their beady eyes were darting left and right for enemies.

Dada plonked himself down, tired from the trek across the hilly meadow. Maldruff scurried around the tree very excitedly, creating a little dust storm. Maggie sat perched on a branch and declared, 'Murf is fine. He is rested but very weak, so will need plenty of Mammy's buttercup soup to get him up and around.'

Dada lifted his weary head and looked at Maggie with his big, saucer eyes. He then shook his head in dismay. 'Dat boglun is goin to be grounded forever. Never will dat little wagglegob be allowed to leave da house again! Where is he?'

Over the limb of the tree, a sorry little face emerged, looking like a squashed tomato. It was Murf with his sheepish grin and floppy, orange hair hanging over one eye.

'Oh, Dada, I'm so sorry,' said Murf. 'I wuz just larking and meself got all bamboozled in Smelly Nellie's room,' he said and sighed.

Dada stood there with his hands on his hips. He shook his head in dismay as he looked up at his hapless son. 'Murf Muklefinn,' Dada declared. 'You's is da silliest of all bogluns in da valley! What were ye at, ye wagglegob?'

Murf again gave a sheepish stare and threw one big, flat foot over the branch and scratched his orange mop of hair. 'I am sorry, Dada,' he replied squeakily, trying to tidy his unruly mop.

Meanwhile, the water weasels had found an old, discarded tea tray near the Mc Nally's rubbish dump and had dragged it back as a

makeshift sledge to pull the weary boglun
back to the river.

Dada thanked the magpies for their
kindness and all gave each other a bogglehug
before plonking Murf on the tea tray. The
weasels had fashioned ivy ropes to the front
handle and set off pulling Murf back through
the long grass. They set off to the river at
tremendous speed, bumping over stones,
with Dada and Maldruff scooting along
behind. The tray shot over the long grass with
ease, with the little boglun grasped onto the
sides with his spindly arms, grinning from ear
to ear as it glided effortlessly through the
meadow.

Finally, they reached the river and little
green boat. The weasels then slid into the
water to attach the ivy rope for the tow home.
Off they set with Maldruff sitting upfront like
the captain. His pink nose sniffed the morning
air as they glided between the bulrushes and

water grasses, pulling the boat back to the safety of Kellerbeg bog and home.

Within no time, the weasels turned the bend on the river and could see the boglun homestead in the distance. Mammy and Twiggle were pacing up and down, awaiting their arrival. Corny had flown ahead to tell everyone of the rescue and that all was well, as the little, green boat pushed in through the rushes. The weasels tied the boat into its mooring and slid off down the river to look for some food. Dada jumped onto the riverbank to help Murf disembark.

Mammy was so excited to see her little boy again. She grabbed Murf and bogglehugged him so tight he nearly fainted. 'Murf Muklefinn,' she cried, 'you's is da naughtiest wagglegob and ditchdragger I have ever set my eyes upon! Now, get into da house and go to your room right now.' Mammy then led Murf by his pointy ear and marched him into the homestead as he squeaked in pain at his mammy's grip. But Murf didn't mind as he was safe at last.

Outside, Dada thanked the weasels for their help, remarking how efficient they had been in carrying out the rescue.

Maldruff leaned against a tree, proudly looking down at his muddy claws and dirty fingernails. He stroked his slimy whiskers with the other paw and barked, 'There is a cost, Dada.'

'Oh yes, yes, I understand,' said Dada. 'What reward doos ye tink is due?'

Maldruff's nose scrunched up as he looked towards the sky. 'You will have to present Murf to the High Lord Grizzle,' he replied.

Dada's fluffy hair stood on end like a gooseberry with fear at the thought of seeing Grizzle face to face.

'There will be payment of dazzle to the lord for our service,' stated Maldruff. 'And maybe more as Lord Grizzle is of a most disgruntled nature lately.'

'Oh?' Dada replied. 'When would he wish us to be comin to him?'

Maldruff stood up straight and looked Dada in the eye. He stared very intensely. 'In time, Dada. In time,' he replied, then slid into the water and swam off, disappearing into the rushes.

Life returned to normal for the boglun family. Twiggle foraged in the woods for toadstools, acorns and beetroots, all to be gathered for Mammy's wonderful stews. Dada collected gooseberries and raspberries to store in the larder for winter. A few days had passed and Murf was confined to the riverbank within cackling distance of the homestead because of his previous adventures. So, he spent his days bouncing around the bulrushes, annoying Gribbo and splashing water at Twiggle every time she came passed.

One morning, Corny flew down with important news. Lord Grizzle had summoned Murf and his father to his lair to answer for his naughty adventure to Smelly Nellie's farm, the crow announced.

The family were very nervous and anxious to hear the news and had to dress in their finest toggles to be in the presence of Lord Grizzle. Murf seemed very relaxed about the meeting and told the family he was not too worried about it. Dada looked at the little boglun in shock.

'Do ye realise dat da High Lord Grizzle will want dazzle from da family, Murf, ya silly wagglegob.'

Murf sat back, grinning his silly smile, then reached into his sack. Lifting the flap, he slowly pulled out a small bag. It was Smelly Nellie's necklace. He had taken it off the mirror in her bedroom. The family sat back in disbelief and shock at the sight of the wonderful, gold, glittering item.

'Oh no!' Dada spluttered. 'Ye took da human girl's dazzle?'

'Yep,' replied Murf. 'Grizzle will be happy wid dat, huh?'

A silence filled the treehouse as the bogluns all stared at the glittering prize swinging from Murf's thin long fingers.

'What will Lord Grizzle make of this then?' Murf sniggered.

Murf meets Lord Grizzle

The time had come for Dada and Murf to make their way to the lord's lair. They set off down the meadow in their finest toggles, with Murf clutching his sack containing the dazzle over his shoulder. The air felt heavy and clammy as he skipped and danced unawares, twirling in circles as they ambled down the hill towards Lord Grizzle's cave.

Corny flew up and scanned the land below and saw a great crowd starting to gather. The river weasels were there and the water rats. Dilly Duck and all her ducklings, plus all the small birds in the area flocked in the trees hoping to see Grizzle emerge from his domain. Dada, however, had a bad feeling about what might happen. This meeting could be full of danger if Murf angered or annoyed the large bog lord and bad things could ensue.

Dada grabbed Murf and gave him a shake. 'Behave, ya scallywag. Ye has never seen da lord high boglun. He is a very scary creature, my boyo.'

As they trundled through the long grass and made their way to the riverbank, the sky turned dark and grey clouds started to gather above the bogland. A fine mist started to fall and all the forest and river animals fell silent and birds stopped chirping, perched silently in the treetops. Dilly Duck's ducklings bundled under her wings for safety and the river dragonflies stopped hovering and settled upon the lily pads and bulrushes, awaiting the spectacle to come.

In the distance, Dada could see the flicker of the tall water reed torches burning around Grizzle's lair. Weasels and rats were lined up like soldiers. Upon seeing this, Murf gulped and tried to swallow but his throat had gone dry. His jumping and spinning stopped abruptly.

Dada gently pushed the little boglun towards the entrance of Grizzle's lair.

'Halt,' Maldruff cried, standing in front of his army of weasels. Their slimy heads darted left and right in the torchlight. 'Upon your knees, Boglun,' barked Maldruff.

Murf fell to his knees as the weasel pushed Dada away from little Murf. Without warning, his large, muddy back foot crashed down upon Murf's neck, pinning his nose into the riverbank mud.

'Do not look upon Lord Grizzle or speak unless he commands you do so. Understand?' the weasel bellowed.

Murf could only nod his head as his orange mop of hair was buried into the swampy ground.

Suddenly, all the weasels and rats started to stomp their feet together on the damp riverbank, making the ground under Murf vibrate. Then they all fell silent.

Within the entrance of the lair, a strange noise started to sound, getting louder like a sack of potatoes being dragged across loose stones. Then dust started to float out of the entrance as the noise increased. The cave was as dark as night and a light breeze started to come from the gloomy tunnel as the sound grew stronger.

Slowly, a giant, dark-grey figure began to fill the lair's opening with a glittering reflection from the light of the burning torches that flickered around the entrance. Slowly, a large gnarly hand with long, black fingernails grabbed the edge of the tunnel entrance and the large, dark shadow filled the space with another large claw grabbing the other side of the cave. With a groan, the monster boglun emerged into the flickering light.

He was a gigantic, gruesome, grey figure, three times larger than a normal boglun. His bumpy skin resembled a frog and his massive feet sank in the mud at the entrance. Slowly, the giant's black marble eyes looked around his domain. His large, puffy lips twitched as his long, black, sharp, iron jaw teeth glinted in the evening torchlight. Upon his massive chest was a breastplate of armour made from jam jar lids all fastened together to resemble chainmail armour, which reflected in the torchlight. On his big, bumpy head, he had a crown made from sheep wire covered with pointed pieces of broken mirror and different coloured milk bottle tops that glinted in the moonlight. He was truly a fearsome figure to behold.

Grizzle spoke in ancient Boglish and his loud, booming, gravel voice sounded over the wetlands as he spoke. 'Who hath come before me?' he bellowed, his voice shaking the leaves off the surrounding bushes.

Maldruff removed his large, muddy foot from Murf's neck and bowed down before the large boglun. 'Oh, Mighty Lord, we bring Murf

Muklefinn as you commanded,' he announced to his master.

Grizzle's black, watery eyes swivelled and looked down upon the helpless boglun. 'Who gave thou permission to enter a human domain without my command?' his deep gravel voice rasped.

Murf's little legs and body shook with fear as the monster boglun stood over him. His black, pointed teeth glinted in the flickering light.

As Murf lifted his muddy head, his body quivered like jelly as he tried to speak. Dada then bowed before Grizzle to try and explain his silly son's antics that fateful day.

'Silence,' Grizzle boomed. 'Let the worm explain himself!'

Murf stuttered and spluttered his story out as all the bog-land animals listened in disbelief, then started to sigh and whisper between each other as Grizzle snarled intensely at the little boglun.

'Enough,' boomed Grizzle. 'You are to make good your foolishness and make a tribute to me. You will present to me two buckets of dazzle and from this day forth, obey the laws of my realm in Ballinalee and Kellerbeg or you will be thrown to the weasels for supper!'

Murf shook his head in gratitude to the Lord of Bogluns and immediately slid his hand into his sack, pulling out the necklace and holding it up to Grizzle.

'Will this be payment, my lord?' exclaimed Murf with a silly grin and glint in his eye.

Grizzle's face changed. His eyes stared down at the necklace held out before him and his eyes started to bulge from his head like big, black balloons. His large, puffy lips peeled back to expose his long, black, sharp teeth with bubbly slobber starting to foam around his mouth. With a thud, the large boglun fell back into his lair, crashing onto his bottom with dust and stones flying everywhere, his jam jar lid armour clanking and jangling as the giant reeled backwards.

Suddenly, Grizzle's large, powerful arm reached out with his long, pointed, black nails and grabbed Murf by his neck and pulled him on to his feet.

'Where doth this worm I hold get this dazzle?' he hissed into Murf's face.

'Oh Lord Grizzle, I got it from Smelly Nellie's bedroom. 'Twas just hanging on her dazzle glass,' Murf shakily replied.

Lord Grizzle stood up and released Murf from his grasp, throwing the little boglun to the ground. All the weasels and water rats whispered and pointed at little boglun who was now petrified.

Maldruff stepped forward and looked at the glittering gem. 'This be the Princess Fannah's!' All the animals sighed and started to growl at Murf.

Grizzle stood silent. His shoulders drooped and his beady, black eyes quivered as he peered at the necklace. Then, slowly, a tear rolled down his grey, leathery cheek as his head bowed forward.

Grizzle lifted his head and with a thunderous roar pointed towards the weasel army. 'Prepare my water chariot,' Grizzle boomed. 'Make ready to march.'

The weasels and rats scurried around in a frenzy in and out of the reeds and riverbank as Murf and Dada sat there bemused as to what had just happened.

'Oh Murf,' Dada harked. 'Tis da Princess Fannah's necklace; da Lord Grizzle's queen. How could it be in Smelly Nellie's room?'

Murf looked bemused. 'Oh goggly. May it of bin takin from her by Nellie and she may be knowin of her whererounds me tinks?'

The silence in Kellerbeg bog was broken. Corny looked down upon the feverish preparation of Grizzle's weasel army and word was sent out to all the boglun clans throughout the land that Princess Fannah's necklace had been found. Now, all must make haste to assemble in Kellerbeg, ready to march upon McNally's farm as the weasels cleaned their baked-bean tin armour and polished their crubeknockers in case of attack by stripeys, barkies or fluffers.

Grizzle cleaned his bottle-top crown and brushed his big, black teeth with tree bark, sharpening his long, talon nails on the river stones in readiness for the trip.

The large boglun then announced that all subjects be prepared by the following sunset, and his wooden water chariot was to be made ready for departure. Corny looked down from the oak tree and shook his feathery head as the mighty army assembled in Kellerbeg.

Finally, dusk fell and Grizzle climbed onto the vessel that bobbed up and down in the flowing river with twenty water rats harnessed and now ready to pull the mighty sledge. All the boglun and weasel army stood in readiness for the command from Grizzle.

'Forward,' cried Grizzle in a booming shout, and the hoards moved off in one large mass like an army of ants. The bushes and reeds in the river shook as the water grasses parted and flattened with the army emerging from the riverbed. The ripples of water turned to waves against the bank as the mighty army moved off into the darkness.

Slowly, through the night, the large army glided through the river towards McNally's farm with the rodents' rusty, tin armour clinking in the chilly night air. As the Kellerbeg and Ballinalee bogluns scurried along the riverbank with their crubeknockers over their shoulders, they kept their eyes peeled for enemies such as stripeys, who normally hunted at night.

Shortly before dawn, Grizzle and his army reached McNally's farm. The large army split up to surround the homestead as Grizzle jumped from his chariot to make the ascent to the farmhouse. Grizzle was not afraid of farm dogs like Buddy and Golly as he was as large and strong, he also had magical powers to rely on.

Around the back of the farm, Buddy the dog was the first to hear something. Buddy nudged Golly. 'Do you hear something?' he said as they both sat up in their kennels sniffing the night air.

Buddy's ears flicked around like a startled rabbits. 'I can smell boiled cabbage and bacon, Golly,' Buddy woofed.

'Huh,' replied Golly, 'what rubbish. That was the McNallys' dinner earlier'

But slowly, both started to feel uneasy. Just then in the moonlight, Golly saw a shadow coming towards him. 'Who's that?' Golly barked.

It was Grizzle, snarling and staring at the pair of dogs with his black, beady eyes. Within a flash, a silver web floated down upon them like mist and they were now frozen. They could not bark, move or even run. Grizzle had thrown spiddywizzle and frozen them solid to the ground.

The large boglun lurched forward, black teeth bared, his black eyes spinning in and out like gyroscopes, hypnotising the two dogs, trapping them in a wizzle web.

The large boglun turned towards the farm building's back door as the weasels and rats stood guard around the farm. Murf and Dada were hiding in the bushes, very scared.

Grizzle sank his sharp teeth into the back door as if it were cheese, his powerful claws ripping away a large hole into the McNally's kitchen. Grizzle grunted as he squeezed his body through the splintered wood, followed by Maldruff, Dada and Murf, both now shaking like flowers on a blustery day.

The large boglun turned and beckoned Murf with his long claw finger and said, 'Where be Nellie's room?'

The little boglun shrugged his shoulders and blinked his saucer-like eyes in confusion as he had never been in this part of the house before. Grizzle pushed passed the trio and started to climb the tall stairs. His large, claw-like feet splodged up the carpeted steps, followed by the others. Once at the top, Grizzle saw many doors. But which one is Nellie's? he pondered.

He opened the first door but it was an empty bathroom. Proceeding along the landing, he opened a second door and within the moonlight, Grizzle could see two bumps in a bed. It was Farmer McNally and his wife Nora, asleep and snoring away. Grizzle jumped like a frog onto the sleeping pair and with a sweep of his arm threw the magic wizzle over them, freezing them instantly in a web cocoon, preventing them from moving. The sleeping pair did not even notice or wake up, so they were unaware Grizzle had even done this.

Grizzle jumped down and proceeded to the next room. Murf had a feeling this was Nellie's as he could smell the pong. Grizzle slowly opened the creaky door and, sure enough, an awful smell of crusty socks drifted out. That is definitely Smelly Nellie's room, he thought.

Grizzle thudded towards the end of the bed, closely followed by the trio. The two bogluns shook with fear as Maldruff pushed them along in the darkness. Suddenly, Murf banged his big, flat foot on the leg of Nellie's bed.

'Ouch,' Murf cried out, wincing in pain.

Nellie stirred and sat up. 'Is that you, Mammy?' she called out in the darkness, but the room was silent. Nellie reached out and turned on her bedside light and with one bound, Grizzle jumped on to her bed, his teeth bared and claws digging into her bedclothes. With a sweep of his arm, Grizzle cast the silvery web over Nellie as she tried to scream at the sight of the monster boglun, but it was too late.

Grizzle's lip quivered and slime ran down his chin as he came closer to frozen Nellie. His hot breath blowing onto her face.

Nellie desperately tried to scream and shook in fear from head to toe at the sight of the monster sitting on top of her. His sharp, black teeth just inches away from her face. Nellie was frozen and could not cry out for help as the silvery web became tighter and tighter the more she tried to struggle.

Slowly, the giant boglun leaned over and whispered in her ear, 'Where dost thou get this?' He was dangling Fannah's necklace in front of the stricken Nellie.

The little girl shook in fear but could not reply because of the web.

Grizzle's long, black, razor-sharp fingernail slowly cut a slit in the web around her mouth for her to speak. 'If you cry out, human, I will tear out your tongue and you will never speak again,' he whispered.

Nellie's voice trembled as she explained that she had taken it from a fairy a long, long time ago.

Grizzle's face screwed up as his lips peeled back, revealing his fearsome black fangs as they flashed in the moonlight. He then hissed in Nellie's ear, 'Where be the fairy queen!'

Dada and Murf knew that if she didn't tell him, Grizzle was bound to eat her. Nellie slowly squeaked out a reply to the monster boglun. 'I locked her in my rabbit hutch in the garden with my rabbits,' she spluttered in fear. 'I… I… forgot about her. She lives in there now, I think?'

The large boglun leaned closer to Nellie, staring into her petrified face. 'Be any harm done to my queen and you will be no more,' he whispered. His black teeth glinting like mirrors in the moonlight. Grizzle then turned and instructed Maldruff to take his soldiers down to the garden to seek out the rabbit hutch of which the human child had described to him.

Maldruff scurried along the corridor and down the stairs into the back yard. He beckoned his troops hiding in the grass at the edge of the garden.

Slowly, weasels and rats started to appear from everywhere, teeth bared and ready to fight anything that came near them. The bogluns stayed hidden though as they didn't like any type of violence or upset. The rats scurried to and fro, looking behind sheds and outbuildings for the rabbit hutch.

Grizzle stayed firmly planted on top of Nellie awaiting word from Maldruff.

Within a few minutes, a cry went out. The rats had found it tucked away in a barn on a shelf, so Maldruff scurried back to tell Grizzle the news.

Grizzle sealed up Nellie's web around her mouth and jumped down following Maldruff to the hutch. He fearfully approached the shed in the moonlight, shaking in distress at what he may find. Nellie had put the fairy queen in the hutch a long time ago and maybe she had died. Slowly, Grizzle climbed up in the darkness. He pushed away cobwebs and cleared the old empty grain sacks to look beyond the wire screen of the hutch, but there was silence.

Grizzle's eyes welled up in tears as he pressed his bumpy face against the mesh fearing his beloved queen, Fannah, was gone. He tapped his finger on the grille of the hutch and slowly, old newspapers and straw started to move at the back of the box as two large, brown eyes peered out from the straw blinking, then shaking and quivering.

'Who's there?' came a voice from the darkness.

Grizzle moved closer to get a better look, then another voice squeaked, 'Who are you?'

The boglun replied, 'I am Grizzle, lord of the bogluns.'

Slowly, the straw parted and a pink nose poked out of the torn newspapers. It twitched in the air with long whiskers covered in sawdust.

'I am Hoppy, the rabbit! Why are you here, Boglun?'

Grizzle then sighed. 'I am looking for a fairy called Fannah who the human child said might be in this cage.'

'There have been different animals put in here and forgotten about,' replied the rabbit.

Just then another pink nose appeared.

'I'm Harriot the hare. I have been locked in here too by the Nellie child.'

Grizzle asked again about Fannah but the rabbit and hare were so excited to see other animals that they jumped about and dust and old newspapers flew everywhere. Hoppy explained that they were fed every couple of days by Farmer McNally's wife, Nora. She would bring fresh water, lettuce and carrots as Nellie had got bored of her pets and had now forgotten about them, leaving her mammy to care for them.

'We were trapped in the field by Nellie, many moons ago!' Harriot exclaimed. 'And have been forgotten by her now.'

Grizzle nervously asked his question again, his voice becoming louder with frustration. 'Do you know of a fairy called Fannah?'

The cage fell silent and both Hoppy and Harriot's ears popped up and their noses twitched as they thought about Grizzle's question. Hoppy scratched her head and Harriot rubbed her furry chin in thought. Both animals stared at each other as if they were hiding a secret.

Grizzle shook the cage in anger and both Hoppy and Harriot shot back under the straw shaking with fear.

'Don't be angry, Mr Boglun,' cried Hoppy from the straw. 'You scare us.'

Sheepishly, Hoppy emerged from her bedding and nervously remarked, 'We know of the fairy Fannah and we have spoken with her.'

'What!' Grizzle exclaimed. 'You have spoken with her? Where is she?' Grizzle asked excitedly.

Hoppy explained slowly and nervously that the fairy Fannah had been put in the hutch many moons ago and was very ill when she had been placed there by Nellie.

'Fannah had been pale and limp, and her beautiful, silk wings were broken and twisted as Nellie had stuck her in an old biscuit tin wrapped in tissue paper and left her,' the rabbit replied.

Grizzle grasped the cage in anguish. 'Tell me more, Rabbit,' he hissed.

'Well, Fairy Fannah told us that she may be rescued one day. She said he will be tall, very handsome and with beautiful, orange hair.'

'That's me!' Grizzle exclaimed.

Hoppy and Harriot then sniggered to each other as they both stared at the large, frog-like, ugly creature in front of them.

'I was once that creature but time has been cruel to me in my search for my beautiful princess.'

Harriot turned away and started to clear the straw from the back of the hutch. In the dim light, a box lay there covered in spider web so thick that it resembled ropes. Harriot explained that when Fannah was placed in there, she lay in the tin very ill and they didn't hold out much hope she would survive.

Grizzle gulped as he tried to hold back his tears at the news. He slumped down in despair.

Harriot then continued the story. 'On the first night she was here, a humming sound came from the box,' Harriot explained. 'This sound continued for a long time and the humming increased. Slowly, hundreds of spiders came crawling into our hutch and spun and spun webs all night around the box making a cocoon around Fannah. We both were told by the largest spider to never touch the box as it had a special ingredient added in the web that would protect her until her prince could rescue her. The humming sound had been Fannah calling the spiders for help, but seeing it was such a long time ago we had given up on her prince ever finding her again,' said Harriot.

Grizzle stood up straight and with one swipe, his large claw grabbed the front of the cage and ripped it off.

Hoppy and Harriot again dived for cover as the cage door flew across the shed and dust and straw flew everywhere.

Grizzle gently reached in, and one by one, lifted Hoppy and Harriot out onto the floor of the shed. 'You are free to return to your homes,' he declared to them both.

Maldruff just sat there aghast, listening to this fantastic story but just could not believe that the fairy would still be alive after all this length of time had passed.

Hoppy and Harriot bounced around on the shed floor with glee, creating a terrible racket as sawdust filled the air. Excitedly, the two friends hugged each other at their newfound freedom and hopped away into the night to look for the burrows where they had once lived.

Grizzle's face had changed, his teeth stopped showing, his lips puckered and his eyes became soft and clear as he gently reached in for the box stuck at the back of the hutch.

By this time, the word had passed around to all creatures that Fannah had been found. All the bog creatures gathered silently around the shed in the moonlight as Grizzle emerged, holding and caressing the fragile tin box covered in spider web. All the animals sighed to see Grizzle's face so changed. His eyes now gently stared at his bundle.

Grizzle strode across the yard, summoning Maldruff to bring the tea tray that had once carried Murf to safety. It would be needed to transport Princess Fannah back to the water chariot.

With Fannah safely placed on the tray, the weasels gently towed it away back down the meadow to the riverbank. Dada and Murf followed closely behind, looking around them as they bumbled back down to the river in the darkness.

Just as Grizzle was leaving, he lifted his arm and swiped the air with his large, grey claw. Suddenly, a white mist started to fall upon the farmyard and, within seconds, the spiddywizzle started to melt away around both farm dogs and the McNally's farmhouse.

Nellie shook herself in her bed, not quite believing what just had happened. She then screamed and ran down the hallway to her sleeping parents' bedroom. She jumped onto their bed, shaking and crying.

Nellie's mammy awoke and hugged her tightly. 'Now, now, Nellie, calm down. You just had a nightmare. Everything is okay.'

'No. No,' Nellie sobbed. 'There was a monster in my bedroom that was going to eat me!' she exclaimed.

'Oh Nellie,' said her sleepy father, 'stay here and go back to sleep. All will be well in the morning.'

Little did they know that Nellie was telling the truth.

THE ARRIVAL OF FANNAH

On the riverbank, they carefully loaded the web-encrusted box and Grizzle guarded the tiny cargo as they pushed off into the night with all the creatures following along the riverbank. The journey was silent as Maldruff led his weasels and rats back to Kellerbeg and home.

Dawn broke as the procession rounded the bend in the river. All the creatures nervously awaited Grizzle's arrival with the princess. As they approached the entrance to Grizzle's lair, Maldruff and the weasels gently unloaded the webbed box. Grizzle carried it into the tunnel and disappeared from sight into the darkness.

Dada and Murf returned home to Mammy and Twiggle who were anxiously awaiting their arrival. They all bogglehugged as the morning sun started to appear above the treetops.

Many days had passed and there had been no sign of Grizzle. The entrance to the lair was cold and windswept. Dada had left acorn buns and a beetroot pie outside but nobody came out to collect the little gift except for the greedy rats that sniffed around. However, they did not dare to take it, just in case Grizzle came out and caught them.

That morning, Corny flew down to tell Dada the news that the human child Nellie was very ill and an ambulance had come to the farmstead. Murf was quite upset to hear the news that she was sickly. Even though she had been very cruel to him and the other creatures, he did not wish any harm to come to her despite what she had done.

'I wuz wonderin if da Lord Grizzle put spells upon her,' Murf remarked.

'I don't know Murf. He may have done as he was very angry,' replied Corny.

The following evening, Maldruff arrived to inform everyone that they must assemble at Grizzle's lair at sunrise. The lord had an announcement to make to the creatures of Kellerbeg and Ballinalee.

The next morning, the Muklefinn bogluns sat down to a hearty breakfast of blackberry buns and nettle tea and, as usual, Murf had to be dragged from his nest under threat of a pot of cold water being poured on his woolly head.

The news had spread and all types of creatures were gathering from the surrounding countryside to make the pilgrimage to the event. Gerty goat and her herd from Clancy's farm in Drumlish, and also Fergal the field mouse and family were all on their way. Butterflies danced in the morning air as weasels and water rats scurried in and out of the riverbank in anticipation of Grizzle's announcement to come. The Muklefinns dressed up in their best toggles and set off along the riverbank.

Upon arrival, a great hush descended across the peatlands as the boglun clans assembled outside Grizzle's cave on the riverbank. The time had finally come and the weasels performed their customary foot-stomping to announce Grizzle's appearance at the cave's entrance. Silence fell over the bog as they listened to the rustling echo from the cave's mouth.

In the murky light, Grizzle appeared, and a sigh of amazement echoed around the creatures as they stared aghast at the spectacle before them. Stood there in the morning light was Lord Grizzle as no one in living memory had ever seen him.

A tall, slim, proud creature standing majestically at the entrance shook his bright orange mane of hair. His skin gave off a beautiful glow as the morning sun bounced from his crystal-clear blue eyes.

'Oh, my goggly,' Murf exclaimed to his father. 'What has happened to Lord Grizzle? He's another creature.'

'He has shape-shifted with happiness, Murf,' said Dada.

'I wish Gribbo would shape-shift into a tadpole,' sighed Murf.

Grizzle started to speak but instead of a croaky bark, his voice had transformed into a melodic, calm tone that transfixed the creatures assembled. He started his announcement by explaining the difference in his appearance and how, by finding his Princess Fannah, his life had magically transformed.

'My life was a wasteland of sadness without my princess,' he said. 'My days rolled from morning to night without purpose to my life, and I became cruel and demanding from my subjects of this fine land.'

Most of the creatures present rolled their eyes and nodded in agreement at Grizzle's comments and Maldruff scratched his chin as he listened to the speech.

Lord Grizzle then threw back his arm and shouted, 'I hereby present before you my fairy princess, the high majesty of the elfin kingdom: Fannah.'

With that, a golden shimmer came from within the cave entrance and a drifting shadow of golden silk floated in the morning air with beautiful, silver, lace wings reflecting light across the faces of the creatures present. She was truly a beautiful being to behold.

Fannah floated like a feather down to the riverbank and landed upon a rock. Her gossamer wings folded onto her back with beautiful, silver, silken hair cascading like a stream over her shoulders. She lifted her ivory-white arm and waved a greeting to the creatures before her. She smiled before settling down to tell her story.

'As you all are aware, I was captured by the human child Nellie and was imprisoned with Hoppy and Harriot for many moons,' Princess Fannah explained. 'I called the spiders of the land to come to me and spin a cocoon of magic silk to protect me. This placed me into an eternal sleep until the day my lord would free me from my prison. Due to the efforts of little boglun Murf, Cornelius and Maldruff, my Lord Grizzle and all creatures present, I now stand before you as your dear friend, and thank you for the kindness and help you all have shown to me.'

Even Gribbo had a tear in his eye as he listened from his lily pad.

'I have heard word from the creatures of the land,' Fannah announced. 'The human child Nellie now lays stricken with human illness and she is slipping away as we speak. I have no anger or hatred toward this human. Although her actions were cruel, I wish to be taken to her and help the girl child.'

All the creatures present started to look at each other in confusion at Fannah's statement. They could not understand why she would want to help such a cruel child.

Fannah then continued. 'In our land, all creatures help and love one another. Even though the human child is not from our kingdom, we must show kindness and love to all living things, despite the ignorance and cruelty in this world.'

Dada jumped up, clapping his long, feathery hands. He was followed by Murf and then all the bog creatures joined in with thunderous applause.

Grizzle bowed to the fairy princess in agreement and then announced, 'I declare free spiddywizzle to all creatures of this land if ever sickness befalls any creature in our kingdom. Also, from this day forth, none will need to collect dazzle anymore.'

Again, the crowd clapped loudly at the news.

'Corny, will you come with me to the stricken Nellie's farm?' Fannah asked.

'Of course, my princess,' Corny replied eagerly.

Fannah leaned forward and kissed the crow on his feathery head, which made his beak blush bright red. Fannah then turned to Murf and stroked his unruly mop and placed the golden necklace he had taken around his neck in gratitude for his efforts.

Murf was ecstatic and bounced around with his prize while all the bog-land creatures bogglehugged him and shook his little hand vigorously.

Nellie meets Fannah

As dusk started to fall, Corny prepared himself for the journey to Nellie's farm and flew down to Grizzle's cave to collect Fannah. The fairy princess emerged and slipped effortlessly onto the large crow's back, placing her slender arms around his large neck ready to fly. Flap, flap, flap and they were up into the evening wind as the pair swirled away on the evening breeze.

Corny had no trouble with the added weight as Fannah was lighter than air on his back. On they flew, upwards over the black turf land and across the fields as darkness fell upon the kingdom. As Corny circled the homestead, Fannah tugged on the bird's feathers and pointed down for him to land on the farmhouse window outside Nellie's bedroom.

Fannah stepped down from the crow's back and peered through the open window. By the dim light of a candle, Nellie's mammy, Nora, sat beside her bed. Her head was resting on the ruffled blankets.

Corny could see Farmer McNally in the distance from the window ledge as he locked in the hens for the night. His head was bowed and there was a great sadness on his face.

Little Nellie lay helpless in the gloomy room. Her face was grey and her eyes were sunken as she licked her dry, cracked lips. Gently, Nellie's mammy patted her fevered brow with a moist cloth, sobbing as she held her hand.

Fannah knew the girl child was wasting away with a fatal human illness and time was of the essence. The beautiful fairy glided under the open window like a feather. Her paper-thin wings brushed passed the opening and then stretched out into a sheet of blinding silver.

Nora lifted her head and saw the wonderful apparition hovering over her daughter. 'Oh, by all the saints,' she cried, 'the angels have come for my daughter,' she said, and broke down in tears at the thought of losing her little Nellie.

Fannah floated over the stricken child on a silver mist and held out a golden cup in her long, slim hand, tilting it over the child. From the chalice, a thin stream of silver nectar dribbled onto Nellie's feverish lips. Then, with a sigh, she opened her eyes.

'Oh Fairy,' Nellie whispered. 'I am sorry for what I have done. Please, forgive me,' she murmured.

Fannah leaned **through the open window** and kissed the child on her forehead. She whispered gently in her ear, 'With this cup I do endow, from the Elfin Nemus and the gods of the north winds, this liquid of wizzle I gift to you. I forgive your wrongs to me and grant you with health and happiness from this day forth.' With that, Fannah glided away through the window and off with Corny into the night.

The next morning, all the McNally family were gathered around Nellie's bed as she was sitting up with rose-coloured cheeks. Her eyes were once again sparkling and a happy smile was on her face.

Nora told all the relatives that an angel had come during the night and cured Nellie, but the family thought she must have dreamed it and needed to see a doctor herself.

Nellie explained to them all that it was not angels but a fairy who had kissed her and cured her sickness.

'Whatever had occurred, it was a miracle,' Farmer McNally retorted with relief. From that day forward, Nellie was never cruel again to any creature and even started a sick-animal hospital on the farm after school to care for all creatures in her townland with great success. Some say she just touches the animals and they are healed. Some say it's magic. But whatever it is, they all get better under Nellie's care.

The boglun townland was happy again. Grizzle had been reborn as the great lord he was with Fannah by his side, and all the creatures carried on with their busy lives. Murf was growing up fast, helping Dada more with the chores of the day and planning his next adventure. Mammy and Twiggle paddled their feet in the cool, healthy Kellerbeg bog at sunset after a busy day. Maldruff still patrolled the waterways checking for barkies, while grumpy Gribbo sat on his lily pad, moaning as normal.

Winter of the Plook

After a long, hot summer, winter had come fast over the boglands of Kellerbeg and townland of Ballinalee this year. The freezing chill cut into the landscape and the creatures struggled to keep warm, as the wintery grip swept over the land. Layers of snow had left the valleys in deep swirls of fluffy snow, constantly shifting like an invisible haze of grey across the bogs. Through the flurries small, white snowdrops poked their heads and fragile leaves up through the marshmallow drifts, looking for warmth as witch hazel bushes groaned under the weight of the heavy fall that draped from their branches. The fields and valleys appeared to have no shape as they all blended like a giant meringue, stretching out as far as the eye could see. The flowing river of Kellerbeg had reduced itself to a trickle. It dipped in and out between the dark rocks that protruded through the icy stream like witches' hats. Gribbo the frog's favourite stone where he usually would sit was empty and just a fluffy cone of sparkly ice had taken his place.

Up in the big, old oak tree, Cornelius the crow was snuggled down in his large nest, surrounded by piles of moss and sheep fluff that he had collected during the summer. He was also very lucky to have Mammy and Twiggle's large, stripy scarf which they had knitted for him the previous Christmas to keep him warm. Corny had made a small window in his nest allowing him to look over the frozen boglands. After all, he was the lookout, postman and messenger for the Ballinalee bogluns and turfland creatures.

The Muklefinn bogluns were all hunkered down in their warm underground home beneath the tree on the edge of the river. Mammy Muklefinn was busy sorting her larder of food gathered during the summer. She had berries, nuts and acorn flour plus many other tasty provisions for the long winter to come.

Dada was busy brewing his giggle juice (beer) as he knew that there would be no chance to go foraging in such a fierce winter as this year. During the summer months, Murf had collected old shoes from the local village rubbish dump and was busy remaking them for his sister, Twiggle, as new winter boots. Bogluns are very skilled shoe and boot makers and always reused sheep wool and old leather to fashion new footwear for themselves, which the bogluns named vamps.

Dada had learned how to make vamps by watching an old cobbler called Dribbler O'Driscoll. Dribbler repaired shoes from his little cottage over the hill near Ballamore and Dada had taught his son Murf to make them too. Dada would snoop up around Dribbler's cottage in the evening and peek at the old man through his window as he repaired worn footwear and bags for people of the townland

and surrounding villages. He would spend
hours watching until Dribbler would finally
turn out his oil lamp and go to bed.

Bogluns often used spiddywizzle dust on
shoes to repair them magically, but Dada had
banned the other bogluns from using it as he
thought it was a lazy way to repair them. The
wizzle should only really be used to heal
creatures who are poorly or, in emergencies,
to repair things. Lately, Dribbler had not been
very well and seemed unable to do anything
due to ill health.

Two days had passed and no one had seen
the old man due to the heavy snow and frozen
land. It was making it near impossible to check
if he was safe. Murf asked Dada's permission
for Twiggle and himself to venture out into the
bleak landscape and up to Dribbler's cottage.
They were concerned about the old cobbler's
welfare.

'What are yous askin me?' said Dada. 'Da
cawld winds and snaw (snow in Boglish) will

boggalise ye both, ya silly nunnyheads. Ye cannot go up to da cottage! You's both should not be up around old Dribbler's house. Look what happened at Smelly Nellie's last summertime. No, I totally forbid it,' Dada grunted.

Murf and Twiggle both looked at each other sheepishly and Murf, with his big kipper foot, kicked a bucket of turnips Mammy had just prepared, before storming off to his room very disgruntled at Dada's response. Murf sat in his bedroom sulking and thinking of what he could do next.

He then thought of a solution and burst into the kitchen very excited and spluttered, 'Dada, can Corny check on Dribbler instead then, if wee's cannot go?'

'Well, I don't know, Murf,' Dada replied. 'Corny is all snuggled down in his nest and not be wantin ye to be bothering him on such a cawld day.'

Mammy then turned to look at Dada with a saddened face. 'Ah, Dada, it will be of no harm to just ask Corny. Just ask?' she pleaded.

Dada finally relented. He allowed Murf and Twiggle to venture outside and call up to Corny in the tree to see if he would fly up to Dribbler's cottage. Feverishly, Murf and Twiggle pulled on their snaw vamps (boots) and fleecy winter toggles (clothes). Twiggle had also made white woollen-type bonnets for herself and Murf called noggeens. They had a pocket built into the top to hide their orange hair bobs, which otherwise would stand out in the white winter landscape allowing hungry stripeys or fluffers to spot them. Murf looked so silly in the noggeen that Twiggle had made, with his little nose and big teeth protruding over the front of his woolly headgear.

Twiggle and Mammy both giggled at Murf as he stood in front of them, looking like a big, fat yeti.

'Stop yous cackling and larping at me,' Murf complained. 'At least I am snug for ta go into da snaw.'

Dada unfastened the large log that secured the oak-tree door and leaned hard to push back the deep snow that had piled up in front of it. With a creek, the door groaned open and a great rush of cold air hit him in the face as he looked at the white mountain of icy foam in front of him.

'Oh, goggly,' he cried as he fell into the large drift.

Twiggle laughed and giggled as they pulled him from the snowy pile – all that could be seen was Dada's two large kipper feet sticking out of the icy mountain. Dada jumped up quickly with a snowy mound piled up on his head like an ice cream cone. Very annoyed, he shook off the remaining slush.

'Brrrr. By jangle, it's cawld,' he said, as he jiggled up and down to get warm. Out into the white expanse, Murf and Twiggle trudged, sinking up to their waists but very excited to see the icicles hanging like giant chandeliers from the snow-laden branches of the tree.

'Oh, Murf. This is bogfabulous. It's like carpets of snawdrops!' Twiggle exclaimed, as her big blue eyes scanned the riverbank.

Murf hurriedly started to climb the slippery hill, promptly disappearing up to his neck in snow. All that could be seen was his noggeen and goofy teeth poking out of the icy drift. 'Help. Help,' Murf shouted, wiggling and twisting as more snow fell upon him.

Twiggle then fell backwards in hysterical laughter as Murf floundered in the white powdery substance.

'Stop yous cackling, muggleguts,' cried Murf. A large snowball then hit Twiggle between her eyes, carefully aimed by Murf for maximum impact.

Finally, they both ascended the snowy bank, steadying each other as they climbed. Bogluns are lucky creatures as their feet are flat and spread out for bog hopping. That's pretty handy for snow too.

Murf shouted up at the oak tree in his high-pitched squeak, 'Corny, are ye dere?'

Then back came a squawk. 'Yes, I am here and quite cosy, thank you very much.'

'Oh, Corny, please wud ya ever be takin a scoot up around Dribbler O'Driscoll's? Wee's worried for him!' Murf exclaimed.

'Oh okay,' came the reply. 'I will fly up before darkness descends.'

'Oh, Corny,' Twiggle then called out, 'why do they call the human man, Dribbler?'

'It's because he has no teeth and dribbles when he speaks,' came the reply.

'I see,' said Twiggle. Twiggle again called out, 'Corny, why has he no teef?'

Corny sighed quietly and his beady eyes looked up to the white, overcast sky.

'Ummm... it's because he lost them in the bog and Gribbo the frog found them and said finders keepers. So now he uses the teeth to smile and try to look important around the townland,' came the response.

'Oh,' replied Twiggle with a giggle. 'Dem's big teef for a frog!' she exclaimed, cackling loudly. 'He would be lookin like Danny da Donkey down at Big Belly Kelly's farm.'

Corny just shook his head in dismay and sighed once again.

That evening, Corny set off from his cosy nest, complete with Mammy's scarf double wrapped around his neck to keep him warm. His large, black wings thudded back and forth as the great bird flew up into the blizzardy evening. Corny looked down onto the white, sparkly, barren land through the speckled sky and scanned the bare trees poking up through the crispy, white foam. They appeared to look like scarecrows with no clothes on in the moonlight. The shadows glinted and sparkled off the frozen landscape like a carpet of diamonds. He could see Dribbler's cottage in the distance and spied a plume of smoke rising from his chimney stack. At least the old man was keeping warm, Corny thought.

As the crow landed, he hopped quietly up to the cottage window to take a peek inside. He noticed that many pairs of shoes had been left outside covered in snow. Oh crumbs, thought Corny. Dribbler has not taken in any of the town people's repairs and all may not be well. He looked through the misty window. The old man was sitting by his fire, huddled in a large, red blanket and quietly smoking his pipe. He looked unwell. Corny hopped around the homestead and spotted large, deep claw-type footprints in the snow, circling the cottage. These footprints were very big and unlike any creature from around that part of the valley.

Suddenly in the stillness of the evening, Corny heard bushes rustle in the crisp night air and sprinkles of snow sparkled down from the branches of a disturbed holly tree. Startled,

Corny quickly took off. His broad wings took him into flight as he peered down on the disturbance. As the trees rustled, a large, dark shape moved quickly into the woodland glade. A pair of large, bright green eyes peered out as a large, cowering shadow moved very quickly into the undergrowth of the snow-covered wood. It caused sprinkles of fine, white, frosty snow to sprinkle to the ground as the object disappeared into the undergrowth and stillness of the night. Corny was quite scared as he flew away, shivering into the evening moonlight and back to his nest by the river.

The Boglun Department of Investigation

The following morning, Corny flew down to the base of his tree and knocked on Dada's oak-tree door with his big, yellow beak.

Bang, bang, bang!

With that, a large pile of snow fell off a branch above, burying him.

'Oh drat!' Corny exclaimed, as he shook off the cold, icy shower from his black, feathery neck.

The door creaked and shuddered as Dada unlocked the heavy, wooden slab. With a lot of effort, he pushed it open to welcome Corny inside. The Muklefinns were all sitting at the table drinking hot nettle tea. They asked the crow if he wanted a refreshing mug of Mammy's brew, but Corny declined, hopped around and sat comfortably on a wooden stool.

'Well, Corny,' Dada asked. 'What news of Dribbler last evening?'

Corny stroked his beak with his large, feathery wing and tilted his head to one side in a bemused look. 'I am not sure,' Corny replied. 'I flew up at dusk as darkness was coming and saw the old man sitting by his warm fire, but he did not look too well. Boots and shoes were piled up outside. I think he requires some help,' Corny remarked. 'I did notice very large footprints around his cottage. They were a type I had never seen before and I heard noises from the bushes. I also saw two large, green eyes peering out at me too so I flew off.'

'Hhmm…' Dada replied, 'dat does sound very scarifying, Corny.'

Murf and Twiggle were sat up at the table and their eyes were as wide as saucers as they listened, staring intensely as the crow told his story.

'Well, what wuz da green eyes and big feet ting, Corny?' asked Murf.

'I'm not sure,' replied the bird. 'I have heard similar tales like this before from the creatures around the village of Cullifad and they have seen similar. It is very worrying.'

'Bejangles,' Twiggle cried. 'Is it a demon, ye tink?'

Dada rubbed his orange beard and paced up and down the kitchen in deep thought. 'Meself is thinkin' that we's needing advice on dis matter and need to speak to da Lord Boglun Grizzle,' said Dada.

'The only problem is Grizzle and Princess Fannah have gone to stay with her father, the Lord High King Nemus of the Northwind, over the winter. They will not return until springtime,' Corny replied. 'We could have a problem and maybe should seek advice from Gribbo as he is telling everyone he is in charge whilst Lord Grizzle is away,' Corny pondered again, stroking his beak.

'Oh no,' Murf sighed, 'not dat green grumbler. He is always croaking to all da creatures that he is da finest and da cleverest and he's just a silly auld frog claiming he's in charge.'

'Do not disrespect your senior creatures,' retorted Dada. 'Gribbo is the eldest in our townland and deserves the respect due to his age.'

Murf's eyes rolled, looking up to the ceiling and then slumped in his chair, sliding underneath the table in dismay.

'We needs ta be setting up a meeting of Kellerbeg creatures ta decide what is to be done,' said Dada.

Corny agreed and suggested they tell the bogland clans and surrounding animals to gather outside Grizzle's cave as soon as the weather improved enough to do so.

Corny set off the next morning to pass on the news. He flew up to Drumlish to warn Gerty, the nosey goat, of the planned meeting. He told her to pass on the message to other creatures in her locality as she was the neighbourhood chatterbox and busybody and best creature to tell if you want news to travel fast. He then went on to the townland of Cullifad to tell Cynthia the sow and her twin piglets, Sizzle and Rasher, of the coming meeting so they could all attend. After a tiring morning flapping around Ballinalee, Corny returned quite chilly to Kellerbeg for lunch and knocked on Gribbo's underground house built into the side of the riverbank. Corny tapped his beak several times on the elderly frog's door but all was quiet and the crow had trouble gaining a foothold on the slippery slope. Slowly, twigs and rocks moved and Gribbo emerged. His big, bleary eyes squinted at the bright winter morning.

'Who is knocking profusely at my home?' croaked the frog.

'It's me, Corny, the crow,' he declared. 'How are you today, Gribbo?'

'I was fast asleep, if you must know and was dreaming of catching mayflies until you disturbed my residence,' he grumpily replied.

'I am sorry to disturb your winter sleep, but I carry important news for the creatures of Ballinalee. Yourself being the elder of our community, I thought I should inform you of a meeting tomorrow to discuss some problems in the townland.'

'Of course, of course,' replied Gribbo as he wiped his watery eyes and stood up straight in a regal pose. 'You will require my expertise and destruction– I mean INSTR-UCTION, I gather.' Gribbo loved to be important and although he spoke Boglish normally, he would try to speak the posh human language to sound clever but always messed it up.

'I am not sure who will be able to attend as the snow is deep but solid enough to travel. Creatures close by may be able to attend,' said Corny.

'Uhumm,' Gribbo muttered. 'Of course, we can only see what happens,' replied the frog. 'What is the problem you seek advice on as I am very knowledgeable and, of course, being the elder you should insult on these matters?'

Corny corrected the frog. 'You mean CON-SULT, Gribbo?'

'Yes, yes, that too,' Gribbo replied, muttering under his breath.

Corny explained his story of Dribbler's cottage and the very large, strange footprints seen around the homestead, which were rather puzzling and worrying. He also mentioned the pair of green eyes he saw, peering out at him from the woodland.

Gribbo stood up even straighter, increasing his regal stature and clasping his arms behind his back. He hopped up and down the snowy riverbank, appearing deep in thought. However, he really didn't have any idea.

'Yes, yes,' Gribbo croaked. 'We need an export on these matters,' the frog remarked, clearing his throat.

'Ex-pert,' Corny replied.

'Yes, yes. Uhmm… that too,' the frog muttered. Gribbo then threw his long, green flipper leg into the air as a wonderful thought entered his silly head. 'We need to insult, uhmm, con-sult, Master Oswald Blatherpus Tawny of Ballinalack! He is the foremost export, I mean ex-pert, on footprints in snow and is very clever. He has attended Owl school and has Owl levels and is of a most edgumacated disposition. I will send word by Polite Patrick, the courier pigeon, to request his presents.

'Pres-ence,' Corny corrected the frog once more.

'Yes, that too,' Gribbo croaked as he cleared his throat once more.

Cynthia Gets Carted Away

Corny returned to the Muklefinns' homestead. He explained his discussion with Gribbo to the boglun family and informed them that the old frog had requested outside help from Oswald Blatherpus Tawny, who was an expert on footprints in the snow.

Murf sat up and slapped his spindly hand to his head. 'Oh naw. Not dat silly Ozzie Owl!' he cried.

'Now, now!' Mammy exclaimed. 'Don't be making cruel remarks about da poor owl. I am sure he is very wise.'

'He's a brown, feathery tweety-bonce,' Murf groaned.

Further up the valley, Cynthia the sow had spoken to Danny the donkey and remarked that she may not be able to attend the meeting due to her being of a very large and heavy disposition and would probably sink in the snow. Danny shuffled his fluffy legs and chilly hoofs in the slushy ice and suggested that he could maybe use his owner's turf cart and transport everybody who may wish to attend. His owner, Big Belly Kelly the farmer, was away so would not miss his cart being borrowed.

Cynthia thought it was a wonderful idea. 'I can bring the twins, Sizzle and Rasher too,' she replied.

'You will have to help put on my bridle and harness, Cynthia, as I can't do it on my own. Plus, I wouldn't mind carrots for me,' remarked Danny. 'There will be plenty of room on the cart, and maybe we can pick up any other creatures on the way too,' said the donkey.

'How splendid. We need to be very careful so as not to be seen by humans though,' sighed Cynthia. 'Whoever heard of a pig steering a cart?' she tittered, wiping her snout with her large, yellow-spotted hanky.

In the meantime, Polite Patrick had flown up to Ballinalack, to the home of the Tawny family who lived in a large barn outside the village. Patrick landed on the snowy roof and hopped along to the hayloft where Oswald sat amongst two large hay bales reading a book, his spectacles perched on the end of his short, orange beak.

'Excuse me, Mr Tawny. A message from Gribbo Bullfrog of Kellerbeg bog, sir. He requests your immediate attention on the matter of strange footprints in the snow, your Owlyness.' Patrick rubbed his cold, pink feet back and forth on the straw to warm them up whilst shyly staring at the floor of the barn and awaiting Oswald's reply.

'Of course, I will attend,' came the answer. 'I know Gribbo's uncle, Tadious Pole. Such a nice fellow. I have nothing too-wit to do here and am only pretending to read this book to seem clever. I haven't a clue what it says as I can't read,' the little brown owl chuckled under his breath.

'Yes, your book is also upside down,' replied Polite Patrick.

Meanwhile, back at Cullifad, Danny Donkey had moved some hay bales into a type of staircase to assist Cynthia in climbing onto the cart with her twins. Firstly, she threw a large, heavy sack on, which made the old wooden cart creak. This was followed by Sizzle and Rasher who hastily jumped around with glee at the impending cart ride to Kellerbeg. Cynthia grunted and oinked, stumbling and straining herself onto the rickety cart.

'Oh my dears, how delightful!' Cynthia spluttered, wiping her brow as the wheels sank into the hard snow with the added weight. The large sow promptly plonked herself at the front with her large sack and the piglets tucked themselves under her tummy to keep warm. Danny looked around in shock as the cart bowed under the weight. Cynthia then turned her large, polka-dot handkerchief into a headscarf for her wintery jaunt, remarking that the cold wind may make her hairdo look untidy.

Off the little group trotted. Danny managed to get a nice little pace going as the cart ambled through the wintery landscape with Cynthia adjusting her headwear as they went. Further up the bog road, a new passenger waited at the roadside. It was Dilly Duck and her duckling gang, shaking the snow off their downy feathers and eagerly waiting for the cart to stop.

'Jump on,' Danny neighed at Dilly, and they all clambered aboard, chattering and hugging each other as the cart creakily rolled off again. The added weight was now making Danny start to huff and puff.

As the short journey progressed, the conversation was all about the strange footprints and Dilly declaring that farmer Mahoney's cat got eaten two weeks ago and only its collar was found, plus she saw a trench in the snow quite near Cynthia's farm.

'Ooooah, deary me, really?' the pig remarked, picking her teeth as she looked out onto the bleak landscape. 'Yes,' she continued, 'I too saw the very same when the piglets had swine flu.' The large sow carried on blathering away, describing the footprints whilst constantly sticking her trotter into the large sack she had brought along, crunching and munching as all the other creatures looked on aghast at the amount she ate. Turnips, carrots, beetroots, broken twigs and old mouldy loaves of bread to name but a few, got gobbled as the large sow burped and grunted her way through her lunch. She did not even ask the other passengers if they were hungry.

Finally, poor Danny pulled up the cart at Kellerbeg just as Cynthia finished the last morsel of food from the now empty sack. Burping loudly as she wiped her snout with her polka-dot hanky, she apologised for the noises she made.

'Oh, deary me, oink, deary me. How delightful,' she grunted.

Rasher and Sizzle were so embarrassed about their mother's awful noises. They were now struggling to get out from underneath her giant belly and poor old Danny never even got the carrots he had been promised.

Dada and Mammy emerged from the oak-tree house and welcomed the new arrivals. Murf and Twiggle unhitched Danny and gave him a big bogglehug for his efforts.

'There is being not many creatures here today due to da snaw,' Dada remarked to the group. 'But Maldruff weasel is here and waiting at Grizzle's cave for ye all.' Maldruff needed to attend as he was the Kellerbeg security at times such as this and had a good knowledge of the townland and waterways around Ballinalee.

Corny squawked down to the arrivals from his tree that he could see Oswald Blatherpus Tawny just flying over Kellerbeg hill so he would be arriving shortly.

FOOTPRINTS IN THE SNOW

Mammy greeted Cynthia with a bogglehug, struggling to get her arms around the large pig's neck. She invited her in for a cup of nettle tea and goodies. Mammy had already laid the table with a large acorn sponge cake and oak-leaf pie laid out on little wooden plates for the others, in case they might be hungry but they had gone down to Grizzle's cave to meet the others.

Cynthia squeezed her large frame through Mammy's doorway, grunting and wheezing as the large sow burst into the small boglun kitchen. Cynthia could not sit on any stools in the room as she would break them with her weight, so she just sat on the floor with her head stuck against the ceiling in the tiny oak-tree home.

'Please, have some cake and refreshment, Cynthia,' suggested Mammy to the pig. 'I will just get you a plate.' When Mammy returned,

Cynthia had devoured the huge sponge, the pie and all the nettle tea that was meant for five people.

'Oh purely delightful, Mrs Muklefinn,' the sow burped, wiping the slobbers from her snout with her polka-dot hanky. 'I must return to the meeting!' she exclaimed and then promptly attempted to squeeze herself back out through the front door, cracking the frame and pulling the wooden hinges off as it collapsed onto the snowy ground. 'Oh fiddledums,' Cynthia remarked as she plodded over the broken door, dragging her enormous belly through the snow like a plough.

Mammy sat on her stool mesmerised to see her whole table of cake and pie disappear in moments. And now her front door was squashed into the snow outside too.

Finally, Oswald Owl came gliding in through the wintery sky and Corny flew down to greet him. Ozzie was carrying scientific footprint-test equipment in the bag he had over his shoulder and wore a strange hat that none of the creatures had seen before. The little brown owl skidded to a halt in the fine, powdery snow and all the creatures dived for cover as he crashed into an icy drift. A cough and a splutter came from the snowy mound as Oswald brushed himself down and cleaned his spectacles for his meeting with the creatures of Kellerbeg.

'Allow me to introduce myself. I am Oswald Blatherpus Tawny of Ballinalack,' the owl announced and then swept his wing across his chest and bowed.

Corny, quite confused, copied the owl with the same gesture and the other creatures did the same, wondering why they were doing it.

Maldruff just stood there, his beady eyes staring at the hapless owl and thinking to himself how silly the fluffy bird seemed. Suddenly, on the riverbank, stones and twigs moved and Gribbo lurched forward from his domain, trying to hop but falling face down on the icy surface.

All the creatures looked amazed at the sight before them. As Gribbo attempted to stand up into a regal stance, he struggled to balance himself due to the fact he was wearing Dribbler's false teeth. These were four times bigger than his wide mouth so they pulled him over with the sheer weight.

'Pleethed to meeth you,' came the sound from Gribbo as his chin hit the riverbank.

All the bogland animals fell into raptures of laughter as Gribbo struggled to compose himself and chuckling filled the air. His bumpy face turned from green to red with embarrassment. Very promptly, Gribbo removed the teeth and threw them to one side as he greeted his guest. 'Oswald Blatherpus Tawney, I RESUME,' announced Gribbo in his posh accent.

'Um yes. Presume, you mean,' replied the owl, quite confused. 'Call me Ozzie.

Everybody else does,' said the owl, pushing his spectacles up his little, orange beak.

'That's fine headwear you have, Ozzie,' remarked Gribbo as he stared at the owl's bright green bonnet.

'Oh what, this old thing? Yes,' replied Ozzie, 'it's the latest fashion. It is called a BALLEE-CLAV-A.' And the little owl gave a twirl in the snow. 'I hear you have problems of strange footprints,' said Ozzie to the creatures.

Dada stepped forward, introduced himself and then explained the previous sightings around Dribbler's cottage. Cynthia then confirmed that she too had seen similar marks around her farm as well. This was followed by Gerty the nosey goat confirming the same.

'We must go and look at these prints,' proclaimed Ozzie.

Corny agreed. 'We will both fly up there and I will show you!' exclaimed the crow.

Off the pair flew into the still, overcast wintery sky. Ozzie with his bag and green balaclava and Corny with his stripy scarf fluttering in the wind, as they disappeared from view over the white snow-covered hill to Dribbler's place. Corny and Ozzie circled the homestead and finally landed in a clearing close to the cottage.

Corny pointed to the prints with his large, black wing, cautiously looking around the area, whilst Ozzie hopped over to examine them.

The owl opened his bag and rooted around inside as Corny's beady eyes scanned the treeline and bushes for any movement. Corny then stared at the owl as he pulled out a stick from his bag and started to poke the strange footprints.

'What are you doing?' asked Corny.

'I am taking scientific measurements of the scene,' replied the owl. 'This, my fine-feathered friend, is a precision measuring device that can tell you all sorts of things.'

'But it's just a twig,' replied Corny.

'How very dare you?' replied Ozzie. 'It's not any normal twig. it's a plook-ometer,' replied the owl.

The crow scratched his feathery head in disbelief as Ozzie continued to jab the ground for clues and hopped about, rummaging around in the snow. Suddenly, a high-pitched shuddering and ghastly squeal came from the trees and a crackle of branches broke the morning silence.

Both birds took off from the ground, startled by the noise and crashed into each other as they started to furiously flap their wings. Up they flew into the air with loose feathers flying everywhere. Ozzie's ballee-clava then twisted the wrong way around so he could not see anything. He spiralled into the morning sky, hooting as he flew.

'I'm blind. I'm blind,' squawked Ozzie, until he realised his balaclava had twisted itself backwards in the panic.

Corny looked around as he also gained height and again saw the luminous, green eyes staring out from the undergrowth. There was definitely something around Dribbler's cottage that was very scary.

Both returned to Kellerbeg quite startled. Ozzie was minus his bag and scientific twig, which he'd left on the ground when they'd both fled.

A PLAN OF ACTION

Upon their arrival, both birds fluttered down to the riverbank as the bogland creatures sat waiting for news. Maldruff was first to question the two feathered detectives.

'So, what did you see, Mr Tawny?' Maldruff asked as he scratched his furry chin.

Oswald spluttered and tweeted so fast that he became all muddled up due to the shock, so Corny had to explain to Maldruff.

The weasel looked around at the other creatures who were sitting there quite scared by the story, not knowing how to respond nor what this creature might be.

Ozzie then composed himself and declared, 'We are dealing with a plook.'

'What's a plook?' Twiggle asked as she bogglehugged Murf in anguish.

A plook is a mythical creature that stalks the land during bad winters, looking for sickly creatures to take away.

'Take away?' Cynthia cried. 'I'll have burger and chips! Oh, you mean eat them? Surely not,' she nervously grunted. The creatures and bogluns were very scared at this news and questioned Blatherpus Tawny for more information.

'Oh, goggly!' Dada exclaimed on hearing the story. All the creatures huddled tightly together on the riverbank and looked around in fear.

Ozzie continued. 'Plooks come from the ancient mists of time. Nobody knows from where but they stalk the land in the snow in deep winter and prey upon sick or injured creatures and take them away forever.'

'Oh no,' Gribbo cried, jumping up in shock, 'not frogs, surely?'

'Frogs, bogluns, door mice and even humans if he can snatch them,' replied Ozzie.

Rasher and Sizzle shot under Cynthia's big belly for safety, as too did Dilly's ducklings on hearing this.

'Are they big?' enquired Maldruff, trying to sound brave as his furry paw punched into the snow.

'All I know is they move extremely fast, are very large, have white, shaggy fur, long, sharp fangs and poison claws. They can also see in the dark.'

'Oh, my goggly gosh,' Murf cried. 'The green eyes you saw, Corny, was a real monsta creature to be sure.' The little boglun's big eyes widened in panic. Murf turned to Gribbo as he was the eldest, most experienced creature in Kellerbeg, but all he saw was the elderly frog's flippers and long back legs disappearing into this house in the riverbank, as he rapidly boarded up his burrow with rocks and stones, leaving the creatures sitting around outside Grizzle's cave.

'A great leader ye are,' shouted Murf to the frog.

A muffled reply came back from behind the burrow. 'You heard Ozzie. Plooks eat frogs. I'm an old frog. I'm a sick frog. I'm not even tasty. I'm slimy and horrible and my chin hurts. The plook would get sick eating me,' came the reply, as the old frog pushed more stones against his entrance.

'We have to have a plan,' declared Maldruff. 'And seeing our leader has deserted us, I should take control of our situation.'

'Yes,' all the creatures replied, nodding their heads in agreement.

'I will alert the weasel army and set up patrols around the area. Corny, Ozzie and Polite Peter can be lookouts from the trees, plus they can patrol the area from the air.'

Cynthia was now getting most concerned about everything and declared that food rations be introduced. Also, she should look after it all in case of a shortage.

Mammy rolled her eyes at the thought of Cynthia being in charge of food and made it clear that it was the bogluns who oversee provisions.

'That's it then,' Maldruff declared. 'We all have our jobs to do.'

Twiggle stood up quite concerned and said, 'What about poor Dribbler all alone and no one to repair shoes or get him food? Da Plook might be munching him!'

'Dat is a problem,' replied Dada. 'Wees must help auld Dribbler.'

'I'm not going up around his cottage!' cried Murf. 'Da Plook will be atein me,' he said as he scratched his woolly noggeen in anguish.

Bogluns are kind creatures and they sat around thinking of a way to help the old man. Dada had an idea. He jumped up, skipping around the little group who were all huddled together.

'Wee's go up to Dribbler's cottage and sprinkle spiddywizzle dust on his shoes. Then humans will collect dem all repaired and may leave Dribbler food,' Dada declared.

'I'm not goin up around there,' replied Murf. 'Wizzle or no wizzle, da plook will eat us.'

'We are going to have to face the plook sometime,' said Ozzie. 'Or we all might be eaten.'

'Are Plooks scared of anything?' asked Twiggle.

The little brown owl looked down his spectacles and uttered a confused hoot but really didn't have an answer. He suggested he should consult his mother, Teresa Theobald Tawny of Ballinalack for advice, as she was the wisest and poshest owl in the townland.

Ozzie took off back home to seek advice from his wise mother owl and promised to be back the following day. Meanwhile, the bogland creatures sprang into action patrolling the snowy landscape for footprints near the Kellerbeg homestead.

Cynthia loaded herself onto Danny's cart, grunting and wheezing, complete with a sack of Mammy's food from her larder to sustain her on the wintery trip home to Big Belly's farm. Off they went with Sizzle, Rasher, Gerty,

Dilly and her ducklings huddled together very worried. They were happy Maldruff's weasels were scurrying behind as security in case of any trouble and would alert any other creatures they might meet on the journey home.

The Muklefinn bogluns didn't sleep very well that night due to the news of the plook. They were lucky to have Corny on watch from his nest above the little family though. The following morning at daybreak, Ozzie returned after telling his story to Teresa Tawny his mother, so he had news for the Kellerbeg clan.

As he landed, Maldruff, Dada and Twiggle were there to greet him. Murf was still in his nest, snoring as the morning sun came up over the snow-clad hill, bouncing sunlight across the valley.

'What news?' said Dada.

Ozzie excitedly jumped about, flapping his wings to get warm after his flight and cleaned his fogged-up spectacles with his feathery wing. He spluttered a, 'Too-wit to woo; how do you do?' before he spoke. 'I had a long chat with my mother, Mrs Theobald Tawny regarding the footprints, and she also confirms that it may be a hog-boo or what bogland creatures call a plook,' Ozzie announced. 'She also thinks it definitely sounds like the mythical, demon creature that came from over the cold north waters in the distant past. She has also informed me that they do not like noise, bright lights nor music.'

'Oh interesting,' Twiggle replied as she tugged on her orange hair bob.

So, the little group hatched a plan of action to see if Dribbler was safe and to get those boots and shoes repaired. Bogluns are terrible collectors of junk, from anything that glitters or is shiny, to old tin cans, dustbin lids or anything they can repair and reuse from the humans' rubbish dumps. They even had an old ironing board they used as a sledge.

As the day carried on, the bogluns and weasels scurried about in the snowy landscape, dragging all sorts of items together. Their plan was to create lots of noise once they reached Dribbler's cottage, and so frighten away anything that may be lurking around the area. They couldn't be seen with all their junk during the day because they might be spotted by humans. They all agreed, therefore, to travel up to Dribbler's after dark. So, the little group assembled at dusk.

THE PLOOK ATTACKS

Corny and Ozzie fluttered about in the crisp night air as the weasels gathered their straw torches to light once they arrive. Twiggle would use old pots, cans plus an old children's drum - also from the dump - to bash loudly and scare off anything around the homestead.

Mammy stayed at home and secured the old treehouse door for safety with a big log, as the little group set off into the cold night air, splodging through the crisp, snowy drifts. Sometimes they would disappear with only their noggeens showing as they clambered the hill towards Dribbler's home.

The night was calm and silent as there had been no snowfall for many days but still an icy grip enveloped the land. The little boglun clan looked up to the stars as a full moon lit up the landscape like a mirror of white. Magical swirls of dusty snow blew up around them as their wide feet disturbed the settled drifts. The little group pressed on, holding hands as they dragged the old pots and drum through the wintery land.

Corny had gone ahead with Ozzie but returned with some worrying news. Dribbler's chimney had no smoke. His fire was cold and the door to his cottage was open with items thrown around inside. There was no sign of Dribbler.

This was very startling and made Maldruff and his weasels stop in the heavy snow. The bogluns stared at each other, shaken at Corny's news.

'We must continue,' said Dada. 'We cannot be leaving the human to da plook!' he exclaimed.

Corny explained that there were many confusing tracks in the snow around the cottage so he could not make out what they may be in the moonlight. He advised the little group to be very careful and to cackle if they saw anything. Bogluns make a cackling sound to alert each other of danger or when they need to tell you where they are, which is a good warning system in case of trouble.

As they arrived, Murf's orange mop of hair was standing on end as it had frozen and poked through his noggeen. So had Twiggle's. Dada was okay as he didn't have much hair left. There was just his frosty orange beard that was glinting with icicles like a frozen holly bush. Maldruff's whiskers were also frosty as he blew hot air on his frozen paws and jiggled in the snow to keep warm.

The silence of the night air was broken as a loud, ear-piercing scream echoed from the wooded glade opposite Dribbler's cottage and the frozen snow shuddered down from the surrounding branches. All the creatures froze with fright as the bushes moved and a large object shot across behind the trees, moving through the deep snow. It was so quick the bogluns could not see it.

Suddenly, another louder scream emitted from the tree line. This time it was closer and Maldruff gulped in fear as the sound grew closer to the little group. Ozzie took off from a branch and circled above, trying to spot the disturbance but only heard bushes and branches crack as the screams got closer.

Corny swooped down into the tree line as the little group froze in terror. The bogluns dropped their tin cans and noise-making tools as they got ready to run as fast as they could. The large crow flew towards the noise of bushes and snow that then erupted like a volcano; the dreaded plook finally appearing from the safety of the trees.

The group turned to see the crow flying down like a bullet to save his friends. *Jab, jab.* Corny's beak repeatedly pecked the large, white thing in the darkness. A large, white, furry claw swooped into the air, trying to strike the crow as it screamed up at the bird, but

Corny was very swift and swooped away, screeching at the little group to run.

Twiggle plucked up all her courage as she shook from head to toe in fear and started to bash the little drum she had. She then started singing as loud as she could.

Upon hearing this, the rest of the group did the same, banging and screaming at the top of their voices.

Maldruff struggled to strike his flint stones together for a spark to light the torches, but the little group would not desert each other and continued crashing the old pots and cans, singing as loudly as they could. Suddenly, Maldruff's torch burst into flame and upon seeing the light, the plook turned and disappeared into the night, amid crashing branches and bushes flattening as the monster fled.

Ozzie Blatherpus was petrified with fear. He sat shaking high up on a branch and twittering about what he had just witnessed. Corny landed next to the little owl to console him. The large, black crow then glided slowly down to the group and landed with a thud in front of them.

'The plook has gone,' Corny crowed quietly and told them they could stop making such a racket. However, Murf continued shouting and cackling out of shock and fear so Dada had to put his hand over his mouth to silence the little boglun.

An eerie calm filled the wintery night as the group all stared at each other to ensure everybody was okay and nobody was missing. Corny sat on the frozen snow exhausted. His feet were folded up under him to keep warm.

Twiggle then rushed over to bogglehug the brave crow but he flinched as she tried to comfort him. In the moonlight, Dada could see the snow was red around Corny. They gathered around the injured bird. He had not got away in time and the plook's claw had hit

the bird in the stomach and badly hurt the
large crow.

Corny's long, black wings then stretched
out as he lay in the wintery night, bleeding
badly from the injury. Twiggle sobbed as she
held him tightly, her tears falling onto his
large, yellow beak.

Maldruff was very upset. He rushed into the
treeline followed by the other weasels. They
were shouting and flashing their burning
torches into the darkness in anger but the
plook had vanished.

'How dare you injure my friend?' Maldruff
shouted into the gloom, as the weasels chased
into the woods, looking for the creature. Their
torches shimmered against the dark, bare,
shadowy trees but thank goodness, it was
gone for now.

Murf and Dada rushed into Dribbler's
cottage looking for bandages to help the
injured crow. They found some handkerchiefs
they could borrow. Twiggle gently bandaged

the stricken bird and kissed him on his feathery head, thanking him for being so brave.

Dada then wrapped Corny in a towel to act as a stretcher to get him home down the slippery hill as quickly as possible. Bravely, the little party set off home through the wintery night. Twiggle was holding Corny's wing and stroking the bird's head as they went.

The weasels made sure the courageous crow was comfortable as they carried him. One weasel was at each corner of the stretcher and down the snowy hillside to Kellerbeg Bog and home they went.

Dada feverishly clattered on the oak-tree door. Mammy unlocked the large, wooden structure to see the group holding Corny in his towel stretcher. They rushed the bird into the bogluns' kitchen. Twiggle was sobbing loudly as Mammy and Dada rushed about preparing hot honey treacle bandages to patch up Corny's injury.

Outside in the snow, Maldruff and the other weasels stood quietly with heads bowed in sadness as Ozzie pushed passed to see his feathery friend.

'What do you think you were doing, Corny?' the owl shrilled out. 'You risked your life to fly into the darkness and face a horrible creature that is so dangerous.'

Corny's eyes opened and blinked briefly as he nodded to the little owl. 'I did it for my friends,' he groaned as his voice faded to a whisper. His eyes closed again.

Ozzie patted his friend on the head as Mammy and Dada quickly prepared a bed for the crow. Murf and Ozzie carried the bird to Murf's bedroom.

'You're safe here, Cornelius,' Murf whispered.

By this time, all of Kellerbeg had heard the commotion and even Gribbo emerged from his house, shaking and swiping the air with a muddy, old stick he'd picked up on the riverbank. He shouted at the moon.

The weasels, in the meantime, had set up camp around the boglun house and would be acting as security guards for the night. Twiggle and Mammy made the crow as comfortable as possible and Dada inspected Corny's injury.

'Oh gabbledum,' Dada sighed, rubbing his orange beard - very worried. 'Corny has been hurt bad. Wee's needing spiddywizzle to heal him quickly or he may not survives da night,' he whispered, so as not to let Corny hear him.

'Oh, Dada,' Twiggle sobbed. 'Please, oh, please, help him. He's my bestest friend,' she cried.

'Oh, don't be worrying, Twiggle,' Mammy replied. 'Dada has wizzle for Corny. He will be fine once he has the potion and some rest.' Then she bogglehugged Twiggle tightly.

Murf and Dada prepared the wizzle that had been left to them the previous summer by Lord Grizzle, as thanks for finding Princess

Fannah. They were so lucky to have the magic elixir in their home. Dada diluted the magical, silver fluid into a gold goblet and a sparkling mist rose from the cup as he stirred the liquid. Slowly, he poured the precious, silver nectar onto the crow's wound and chanted a Boglish rhyme. 'Oer thee lords of da wind dat brings us light, maketh thine crow to health and flight,' and with that, they left the crow to heal for the night. Twiggle would sit by his bed, holding his wing 'til the morning came and praying to the fairy lords for his safe recovery.

THE BOGLUN REVENGE

Morning had come and nobody in the Mucklefinn household had really slept that night. They were very worried about Corny and were constantly checking on the sick bird as he lay motionless. Dada had been worried because a plook's gnarly claw was poisonous. He just hoped that the wizzle was powerful enough to cure Corny.

Just then, Twiggle came skipping into the kitchen, crying out, 'Corny's awake. Corny's moving.'

All the household jumped around, hugging and laughing with glee at the great news.

'Phew,' Dada remarked. 'Wees had a close one dere, to be sure and I doos not be wantin to do dat again,' the boglun said and sighed.

All the creatures assembled outside. Maldruff was so happy to hear the news as was Gribbo. The elderly frog hopped about like a breakdancing teenager at the good news.

'I knew the wizzle would work!' Gribbo exclaimed. 'No doubt at all. I know these things as I am very inexperienced in these tatters, you know. Ahhemm,' Gribbo croaked, clearing his throat.

Murf looked at Gribbo and shook his head. 'Yous is a green, croaky, auld gabblegob,' he said and threw a snowball at the frog, hitting him squarely on his bumpy, green head.

'How dare you strike a senior frog of this townland, you spindly bog-hopper!' cried Gribbo, wiping the snow off his nose.

'Now, now, Murf,' Mammy cried. 'I have told ye before; stop yous cackling at Gribbo. He is old and gets confused at times. Please be kind, Murf, at this happy time that Corny is getting better.'

'He's a green boggly-headed lily hopper,' replied Murf begrudgingly.

Corny was sitting up and had drank some nettle tea but was too weak to move. Twiggle made him as comfortable as possible with moss and fern-wand pillows she had made over winter, propping him up in bed to cuddle the crow.

This was now a serious situation that the bogluns and creatures were facing since Cornelius had nearly been taken by the plook that night. Dada thumped around outside his treehouse with his crubeknocker, bashing the snow off the hazel branches in thought.

Dada asked Ozzie if he would take Corny's place as lookout and messenger whilst the crow got better and the little owl agreed.

'We needs help from outside,' said Dada as he paced up and down the riverbank. 'Wees needing more bogluns.'

Maldruff agreed.

'Wee's will send Ozzie with messages to the northern clans and Lord Grizzle. Dere is at least twenty more boglun families dat wud help,' Dada declared. With that, Ozzie took off into the morning mist, heading north to the other clans to pass on the word for action. This was a mighty task that Ozzie was undertaking. The northern bogluns never assembled as an army unless their land or lives were threatened. They also normally needed the permission of Grizzle, the Lord high Boglun and Nemus of the Northwind, the king of the elfin kingdom of Erin.

Ozzie headed north, flying high above the wintery landscape. He checked his little compass as he flew high into the clouds with the message for the clan bogluns. He stopped and rested many times on his flight to check he was heading in the right direction, as Oswald was not a fantastic navigator. Finally, he reached Dun Na Ri Forest to seek out the woodland bogluns.

Ozzie flew down and settled on a snowy branch. He hooted into the quiet wood with a boglun cackle to alert the secretive creatures from their winter burrows. After some minutes, bushes rustled and snow fell from the dense woodland branches as small green objects started to dart back and forth under Ozzie's tree.

Very soon, cackles were echoing around the woods as snow moved and creatures started to shoot about under him. Suddenly, on a branch beside him, a strange-looking boglun appeared. He stared at the owl confused at how he could cackle like one of them.

'Who's you?' the fearsome-looking boglun cried, hanging on to the branch with his spindly arm. He was very nervous to see a cackling owl.

'Hi, I am Ozzie the owl,' he politely replied, lifting his wing in friendship. 'I have flown from Kellerbeg Bog and Dada Mucklefinn to seek help on the matter of a plook,' the bird retorted.

The boglun jumped back on hearing the word plook and his black, beady eyes widened at the name. 'What plook? Ya mean a hog-boo? Where?' he said as he scooted up and down the branches quite startled. The boglun then scooted down the tree in a flash and signalled Ozzie to follow him to the ground and into a clearing in the wood.

OSWALD BLATHERPUS TAWNY MEETS THE WOODLAND BOGLUNS

Ozzie was quite bemused but followed the boglun as he scampered in and out of bushes and trees before finally darting down into a frosty hollow. The ground seemed to be alive with these creatures as they appeared from all directions in the woods. The icy branches shed their snow as these super-quick bogluns darted about in the undergrowth. These bogluns were different from the Ballinalee clan and they also looked strange and scary as Ozzie was to find out.

Ozzie landed in the clearing. He did his customary bow and nervously introduced himself to the creatures, sweeping the loose snow off his shoulders and pushed his spectacles up his nose to have a good look at these strange creatures. The largest boglun jumped down in front of Ozzie, cackling to the rest of the group and then sat in front of the little owl.

'I'm Finn Muddylug, clan cousin to Dada,' announced the large boglun. 'And this is my brother Biffy,' he said as he scratched his long, pointed ear. 'What news of Kellerbeg and a hog-boo, you say?' exclaimed Finn.

Ozzie explained the full story of the past few days to the group as they sat quietly and stared intensely at the owl.

Finn then called his brother to come closer. 'Come you here, Biffy,' he cackled and with that, the other boglun shot over and perched in front of Ozzie. He ogled at him confusingly with his black, beady eyes.

'Oh? Biffy you seem to have a black eye,' remarked Ozzie nervously.

Biffy just shrugged his shoulders and grinned foolishly at the owl.

'Biffy has been fightin and noggin-knockin!' Finn exclaimed.

'What does that mean?' Ozzie enquired.

'It's when young bogluns fool around and bang their heads together for fun,' replied Finn, rubbing his black, tufty head in despair. 'Biffy is only one hundred solars old,' cackled Finn. 'So, he will grow out of it,' he said and sighed.

'Forgive my owlish curiosity but what age are you brothers? You seem young,' enquired the owl.

'I'm older than him,' came Finn's stern response. 'I am two hundred solars.' (Solars are years in boglun terms and most live to be four hundred.) 'Wee's battled plookies or hog-boos before,' explained Finn as his brother Biffy sniffed and playfully biffed Ozzie on his wing in agreement, dislodging his spectacles. Then Biffy progressed to pick his short, stubby nose in boredom.

'Wee's forest bogluns as you can see and wee's different.'

'You certainly are,' replied Ozzie, correcting his specs. 'Biffy certainly lives up to his name.

Bog bogluns are a dappled colour with big, blue eyes and orange bobs of hair. But you bogluns are light green, a bit taller and have black eyes and hair and larger ears. Very different,' the owl declared.

'Wee's are descended kinfolk of the High Elfin Nemus of the Northwind and look more elf than boglun, but wee's the same clan underneath. We are named black bogluns cos wee's have black eyes and wee's tuffy-battle bogluns not softy Kellerbeg ones,' cackled Finn, as he proudly stuck out his chest.

'Oh, I do not disbelieve you, Mr Muddylug,' Ozzie replied nervously. 'As I have explained, I need to seek help from the Boglord Grizzle and the Elfin King Nemus to rid our townland of the plook,' the owl said.

'You will have troubles there!' exclaimed Finn. 'Da high council of Elfin and Pixie chieftains from every locality are meeting in da northlands for the solar gathering in the Gleann Ri Na Siog (Valley of the Fairy King), and dat is of great importance to our future. Looks like yous are stuck wid us forest folk. So, seek ye no further, owly bird,' Finn sniggered. 'Wee's battled plookies in times before humans trod our lands, so wee's know how to hunt them. No need to be bothering Grizzle or King Nemus. Wee's will meet you at Kellerbeg in two sleeps time and we are many,' the boglun replied.

Ozzie thanked the forest bogluns. He started his journey back to Kellerbeg with the news that help was on its way thanks to Finn and brother Biffy, the black-eyed bogluns of Dun Na Ri Forest.

These bogluns were very strange; not only in appearance but they lived differently. Also, although they understood Boglish they spoke human and elfin too. The forest bogluns lived under and above the ground in trees, hence their colour, larger ears to hear and the way they dressed. They wore dark-coloured-type clothing made from wood bark as they could not change colour like their bogland cousins. Their eyes were small and black because of the shady forest they lived in. They also had no rivers or bogs locally so didn't mix much with other animals or creatures. They avoided humans and were slightly more aggressive in their nature, as Biffy showed.

After two stopovers, a big sleep and many snacks, the little brown owl arrived back at Kellerbeg very tired and cold. His spectacles were frosted over with the icy winds he had just flown through and he was grateful to be back in the townland of Ballinalee.

Murf was first out to welcome Ozzie and brought him inside the oak-tree house for supper. Mammy and Twiggle greeted the bird with bogglehugs and a bowl of wood ant and turnip soup, which was Ozzie's favourite.

Dada thanked the owl for his help and Corny crowed hello from his comfy bed, as the owl explained Finn Muddylug's plan.

'Dat is a very scarifying plan that Cousin Finn has to chase off the plook. Mind yous, my cousin is a wee bit blonkerfied! (Nutty in Boglish),' replied Dada.

'Finn said there will be many bogluns and to be ready in two sleeps time, he told me to tell you,' Ozzie tweeted, shakily pushing his spectacles up his little beak.

Dada called in Maldruff and explained what was going to happen. Upon hearing this, the weasel was also apprehensive at such a course of action.

'It could be very dangerous, hunting a plook in snow. After all, if he could take away a human, he wouldn't have any trouble with weasels and bogluns,' Maldruff remarked.

'We have spiddywizzle,' Murf cried. 'We can freeze him.'

'Don't be a silly nunnybonce,' Dada replied. 'You's wud have to be close ta him to doo's dat,' Dada retorted, shaking his head.

The next morning the sun was peeking through a grey sky, and the air was damp with a crispy bite that would freeze noses in seconds. The bogluns and weasels prepared their fire torches and crubeknockers and Murf made a shield out of a saucepan lid. He then went on to constantly bang it with his crubeknocker and fight with a lump of icy snow that hung from a bush.

'Take dat, plookie monsta. Take dat,' he said as he stabbed the snow. The racket Murf was making woke Gribbo who stumbled from his house on the riverbank, very humpy.

'What are you doing, you spindly bogtrodder?' Gribbo croaked angrily.

'I'ms fightin da plook and capturing him, yous auld, green, crockety, bumpy chops,' replied Murf with a giggle.

'What are you incinerating? You couldn't catch a cold or even knock snow off a rope,' croaked the disgruntled, old frog in his broken human language. 'I'm retorting you for infamabordimation,' he croaked at Murf.

The little boglun ignored Gribbo's insults and carried on crashing and banging the snowy mound until his nose went red with frost. He then shot back into his house, shivering.

The day passed with preparations being made all over the boglands. The weasel army started to gather from surrounding areas and the black bogluns, under Finn's command, set off for Ballinalee armed with ash-tree bows and arrows, ivy vine nets, crubeknockers and catapults that the woodland bogluns called slingos; all set for the mighty battle. The northern black-eyed bogluns also had secret allies in the form of a parliament or group of magpies that were also flying up to Kellerbeg as bomber command, to drop rocks into the trees to try and hit the plook when the time came. This was going to be a military

campaign on a military scale with ground and
air support to rid Ballinalee from their demon.

The Battle of Kellerbeg

The day had arrived and creatures from everywhere tried to help prepare for the impending battle. Mammy was very worried as to what may happen and asked Maldruff to look after Dada and her two young children, Murf and Twiggle, as they prepared to leave that evening.

The day was grey and snow had fallen the night before, covering any tracks or pathways that the creatures had cleared. They were going to have a tough time, therefore, climbing the snowy dunes up around Dribbler's homestead and surrounding woods.

As dusk fell on the white carpet of land surrounding Kellerbeg, Ozzie sat in Corny's nest, watching out for intruders and the arrival of the forest bogluns. Suddenly, Ozzie spied a stream of light appearing over the snowy hill. It was the torches of Finn and the northern clan. Their lights stretched out into the distance. It was the black boglun army, approaching through the ice cream snowdrifts.

As Ozzie looked into the sky, he could see the clouds starting to dapple with black and white objects. Pushing his spectacles up his beak, he could make out they were birds; a huge number of birds!

It was the magpies, flying in groups, breaking through the clouds and descending on Kellerbeg. Ozzie fluttered and spluttered as he tried to alert all the creatures below. He flew down to the ground, hooting, squawking and spinning as he tried to speak.

'They're here. The- the - they are here,' he squawked repeatedly. 'Zillions have come. Okay, not zillions but quite a lot,' he tweeted, increasing his hoots. All the creatures started to hurriedly pack equipment as they scampered about, collecting fire torches and sticks for protection and the impending march.

General Gribbo emerged from his riverbank domain, wearing an eggshell helmet and shaking his muddy baton stick convinced he was going to be chief of the boglun army. He hopped up and down, practising his salutes, then started croaking orders at the moon.

Maldruff quickly reminded the old frog that plooks love eating frogs.

In a flash, Gribbo disappeared into his burrow, discarding the eggshell helmet and stick on the damp snowy mound as he fled. He croaked and grunted as he hurriedly filled his doorway with rocks and sticks. That was Gribbo's military career over and done with.

The black bogluns came over the hill and Finn cackled and waved to Dada as he arrived at the meeting point. The boglun cousins bogglehugged as Murf and Biffy proceeded to noggin knock each other in true teenager fashion.

The cousins were very pleased to see each other after such a long time and the rest of the bogluns cackled greetings to one another in the cold night air. Before continuing up to the woods and Dribbler's homestead, the magpies had gathered and sat perched in the snow-laden trees. Dozens of beady eyes watched and waited for further instructions from Finn, cleaning and grooming their feathers after the frosty flight down to Kellerbeg.

The time had come and a plan was agreed. Finn cackled up to the trees to alert the waiting magpies as the land army moved off into the chilly night. Some of the smaller bogluns hitched rides on the weasels' backs as they disappeared into the frosty mist.

The boglun plan was for the weasels to surround the wood with their reed torches to illuminate the forest and the black-eyed bogluns to search the undergrowth for the plook as their eyesight was better for dark woodland. Once spotted, they would signal the magpies to bombard the area, dropping rocks and stones to drive the creature out and then attack it with noise and weapons if it attacked any of them. But ultimately, the plan was to scare the creature away forever at any cost.

Dada led the bog bogluns, including both Murf and Twiggle who stuck close together as they ascended the snowy hill. They pushed through the drifting landscape under the clear night sky, brandishing their crubeknockers and saucepan lid shields as they clambered the powdery surface. They sank and held onto each other as they climbed higher.

Finally, at the top, everyone was quite tired and fearful of what was to happen. The black bogluns spread out and gathered at the edge of the woods. The Kellerbeg bogluns assembled on the other side to block the plook's escape if it came that way. The weasels finally assembled. They lit their water-reed torches on the edge of the forest and spread out as the light illuminated the lonesome woodland branches, casting shadows from the bare trees like cowering witches in the snow. It was truly a haunting place.

All the creatures stood still and silent, listening for any sounds as their eyes scanned the tree lines, but nothing stirred in the cold evening air.

Finn cackled up to the magpies who were carrying rocks and stones. He told them to fly over the woods and call out if anything moved in the bushes and to alert them of trouble. As the tops of the trees rustled, a thudding drone of noise emitted as all the birds took flight at once. Their wings flapped back and forth furiously to gain height over the wooded copse. They constantly scanned the ground for signs of movement as the bogluns stood with weapons and shields, preparing to run into the dark forest.

As the weasels started to move into the woods with their torches held aloft, a crunching noise came from the far corner of the glade. The weasels turned their flickering flames towards the sound. With an almighty crash, the bushes buckled and snowy plumes flew into the air as the silence was broken. The ground shook as a tall, dark shadow darted quickly from behind a tree. It was moving very fast as the creatures tried to pinpoint the direction.

Suddenly, a magpie cawed down to the ground as it flew in under the snowy canopy, dropping its stone bombs into the darkness of the forest. This was followed by an ear-piercing scream. The plook had broken cover and was heading towards Finn and the black bogluns.

All the creatures started to shout and clatter their pots and cans as they moved in towards the disturbance. The black bogluns readied their bows and arrows in anticipation. Dada had brought a spiddywizzle concoction for the bogluns to dip the arrowheads into, which he hoped would help paralyse the plook. He could not be sure, however, as he did not know the size of the creature they were dealing with. It was guesswork if it would be successful or not.

'Fire,' cried Finn, and a volley of arrows and stones from the slingos flew into the air and descended into the darkness as flurries of magpies bombarded the canopy of the woods with stones. Some bogluns started to set fire to the arrow tips as they let loose the repeated shots into the darkness, trying to light up the area. The noise was intense as both the Kellerbeg and black bogluns advanced into the wood, cackling commands to each other as they bravely scurried towards the foe. The weasels darted in and out between the trees with teeth bared and claws out for the confrontation.

Within a matter of minutes, the plook ran out into a clearing and swiped his massive claws at the overhead bombardment of stones. The massive white beast was screaming death-curdling cries at the oncoming bogluns as it kicked out at the weasels trying to bite its hairy legs. The plook's glowing, green eyes swept around, looking for an escape route. His eyes turned a misty red as he constantly smashed the branches. Snow flew in all directions as the giant, hairy monster screamed louder. His long fangs snapping like a crocodile at the barrage of arrows that bounced off his giant, furry torso.

Swooshes of sound echoed through the freezing air as the giant, razor-sharp talons flashed in the moonlight, blindly swiping out his attackers, knocking them away as they rolled and somersaulted. They continually crashed into the snowy, frost-drenched bushes but got up again and repeatedly hit out with their crubeknockers, making the plook scream in pain.

The fight seemed to be going on for hours but it had only been minutes. Shockingly, Murf noticed the arrows were not sticking into the beast because of his thick winter fur. Murf grabbed a wizzle-poisoned arrow and, followed by mad, little Biffy, they both burst into the clearing, darting and dodging the plook's swipes as he reeled in anger at the attack.

As Murf got closer, he knew he would not be able to pierce the heavy fur coat but saw his large, bare, clawed feet. He dived at them in the snow and thrust the arrow into the plook's exposed foot. The hairy monster screamed in agony as he struck out at little Murf, but Biffy blocked the creature's massive, crushing claw, hitting out at it with his crubeknocker to distract its attention. This allowed Murf to scramble away through the bushes. Finally, the plook's giant body crashed to the ground as sweeps of snow billowed into the noisy night air.

Rapidly, both boglun clans and weasels threw everything they could at the plook as it rolled around in the cold night, reeling in agony as the magic wizzle started to paralyse his leg.

The black and Kellerbeg bogluns continued attacking the injured giant as it swooshed and swiped out at its attackers, screaming and howling as the bogluns relentlessly fired their slingos at the monster. This was followed by Maldruff and the weasels snarling and hissing as they prodded their flaming torches at the floundering demon.

Slowly, the plook rose from the slushy ground, its towering body started to limp away, continually blocking the barrage of stones and blows from the boglun crubeknockers. The hairy, white giant dragged its damaged leg through the deep snow attempting to escape. The bogluns were now winning and continued the onslaught at the now-crippled beast.

Dada, seeing the monster was hurt badly, jumped out in front of the boglun army and shouted, 'STOP.'

With that, the creatures ceased attacking the crippled plook as it dragged itself away into the woods, groaning in pain.

Maldruff shook his flaming torch at the hideous creature and shouted out into the dark, gloomy trees, 'Don't you ever come to our lands of peace and happiness again! The next time you will never leave.' He hissed, 'Be warned plook and any of your kind.'

'Yeah, plookie,' shouted Biffy.

A big cheer echoed around Dribbler's cottage as the creatures jumped with joy at their victory that night. They all bogglehugged, threw snow into the air and somersaulted through the white, powdery mounds as they clattered and banged their tins. They cackled in delight at driving away the creature-eating demon. The battle had been won.

Slowly, the bogluns and weasels turned and filed away down the hill, battle-weary and bruised, and back to Mammy in Kellerbeg. Murf and Twiggle linked arms with Dada as they trudged through the night air. Murf and Biffy tried to noggin knock their heads together and tumbled and cackled as they plodded through the icy night.

Mammy was overcome and cried with delight as she saw her little family appear out of the mist on the riverbank, clambering down the icy slope. It could have been a far worse outcome if Murf and Biffy had not stabbed the plook with wizzle. They were brave little heroes that night.

Fires were lit all around Kellerbeg and Mammy and the other creatures had food and giggle juice for the victors, who were singing

old fairy songs and dancing around the flames
'til early morning. They only went to sleep
because of exhaustion and the long, long day
before.

Morning came quickly and slowly the
creatures emerged, bleary-eyed and tired.
They sat in front of the smouldering fires from
the previous night, scratching and preening
themselves. Finn and his bogluns wearily
packed up their belongings and made ready
for the journey home.

Dada and Murf bogglehugged their life-
saving cousins. They thanked them for helping
to rid the monster from Kellerbeg and
promised to visit as soon as the weather
improved in the springtime.

The merry band of black bogluns set off
home, waving and bouncing into the distance
as Ozzie, Dada, Mammy and Twiggle waved
goodbye to the little army. They were quite
sad to see them go so quickly.

Polite Peter the pigeon also had good news. He announced that he had gone with messages up to Cullifad. There, he had been informed by nosey chatterbox Gerty Goat, that Dribbler had not been taken from his cottage by the plook. His family had collected him and had taken him to their home to get better. He would be returning to Kellerbeg very soon.

Twiggle was overjoyed at the news. She excitedly suggested they all go up to Dribbler's house and clean it from top to bottom to welcome him back. Plus, they could repair all his shoes that they had been meaning to do before the plook had come.

Dada thought it was an excellent idea and the little group headed back up to the cottage, dragging hazel twig brushes and brooms plus Mammy's special cleaning fluid that had a splash of wizzle in it for a sparkling effect.

DRIBBLER STOPS DRIBBLING

The snow had stopped and there was a thaw on the way. The icy canopy slowly receded and the river started to turn from a trickle to a torrent as it gained momentum down through the craggy rocks of Kellerbeg.

Gribbo had emerged from his turf house on the river and was sitting on his favourite rock that had been occupied by a large cone of ice only two days previously. He stared into the flowing water, looking for something tasty to eat as he muttered to himself.

Murf slowly sneaked up behind Gribbo and greeted him with a big slap on his slippery back, making the frog splutter. He cackled with laughter as the frog jumped into the freezing water with shock.

'You spindly wagglegob,' cursed Gribbo as he swam back out of the river, shivering.

'How's ye, dis fine morning, greeny chops?' Murf asked, giggling at the frog as he floundered on the riverbank. Murf darted off quickly before the frog could get revenge and ran to catch up with the family, which was setting off for Dribbler's cottage.

Mammy scolded the little boglun for persecuting the disgruntled, old bullfrog. 'Things are certainly back to normal,' Twiggle exclaimed as they all cackled with laughter.

Once up at Dribbler's, Mammy and Twiggle set to work cleaning, brushing and polishing everything with wizzle to a sparkling shine. Murf and Dada heaped all the wet, damp shoes and boots in a pile at the front of the cottage. Dust and spider webs flew out of the cottage into the garden as the little duo inside feverishly scrubbed and polished everything in sight.

Outside, Murf wheezed and puffed as he dragged boots and shoes over to Dada to sprinkle spiddywizzle on them. They then miraculously transformed into sparkling new footwear as the leather and new soles gleamed in the morning light. Murf furiously stacked them back against the cottage wall by the front door, as Twiggle polished the door knocker with wizzle, admiring her reflection as she made it gleam with a golden sparkle. The bogluns were going to town on Dribbler's abode.

Finally, they finished their chores. Twiggle folded Dribbler's blanket and left it by his fireside chair complete with a little wooden box tied with a water-reed bow on the cushion for the old man's return.

A day or so passed and Dribbler's family brought him home, expecting a big spruce-up operation to settle him back into his house. Instead, they were amazed at the cottage. It looked like new.

Dribbler's daughter stood in the doorway, amazed at how clean and tidy it was. She complimented her father on the cleanliness of his cottage.

'I didn't know you had it in you, Dad,' said Dribbler's daughter as she ran her finger over the sparkling surfaces looking for dust.

Dribbler just grinned his gummy smile and sat down in his chair to inspect the strange box tied with a bow. When the family had left, he settled down by his turf fire and slowly opened the strange little box he had found on his seat. 'Yippeeee,' Dribbler cried out as he peered inside. It was his long-lost teeth. Twiggle had rescued them after silly Gribbo discarded them on the riverbank She had wizzle-polished them to a gleaming lustre.

Dribbler was ecstatic as he fitted in his new gnashers and admired himself at every angle in his shiny mirror. He spent the evening grinning at everything he saw with his sparkly new smile. Dribbler knew it was magic at work as he inspected his gleaming, repaired shoes and spotless house.

'It can only be fairy folk,' he muttered to himself, munching a bacon sandwich with his new sparkly teeth. Dribbler stared through his misty window as he puffed on his pipe that evening. He looked at the shadows that danced across the wet, thawing leaves on the edge of the quiet wood and wondered what sort of creatures had been in his home whilst he was away. He imagined little, white-winged fairies fluttering around his house with rags and polish, cleaning everything. Dribbler drew a heart on his misty glass window to say thank you to his kind magical neighbours, hoping they may one day see it.

Little did he know that it was thanks to the Muklefinn and Muddylug bogluns and the battle that had taken place right outside his quiet little cottage just two days previously, just may have saved his life.

Back in the cosy oak-tree house, Twiggle chuckled as she told Murf she had found and returned Dribblers teeth.

'Wee's will have ta call him Smiler O'Driscoll now,' Dada cried out with glee. Corny was nearly back to full strength too. He flapped and fluttered his wings in the boglun kitchen, knocking Mammy's plates off the shelf.

All was good in Kellerbeg once more and Dribbler would not forget the kindness of his neighbourhood bogluns. Perhaps he would be able to return the favour one day.

The end

Illustration by Aneesa Cassimjee.

John Hughes

Dedication

This book is dedicated to Jamie and Ella.

Author Biography

John Hughes is an author who lives in London and Co. Longford Ireland and researches medieval history and Celtic folklore, and he and his children have spent many happy summers exploring the mystical bog lands and wonders of the Irish Lake District.

You can visit his website:
www.johnhughesauthor.co.uk

Acknowledgements

The publishers and authors would like to thank Russell Spencer, Matt Vidler, Susan Woodard, Aneesa Cassimjee, Candida Bradford, Cheryl Mulhair, Martina Cooney, Shelly-Ann, Ben Hughes, and Nathan Hughes, Leonard West, Lianne Bailey-Woodward, Laura Jayne Humphrey and Katie Major for their work, without which this book would not have been possible.

About the Publisher

LR Price Publications is dedicated to publishing books by unknown authors.

We use a mixture of traditional and modern publishing methods to bring our authors' words to the wider world.

We print, publish, distribute and market books in a variety of formats including paper and hard back, electronic books e-books, digital audio books and online.

If you are an author interested in getting your book published; or a book retailer interested in selling our books, please contact us.

www.lrpricepublications.com
L.R. Price Publications Ltd,
27 Old Gloucester Street,
London, WC1N 3AX.
(0203)0519572
publishing@lrprice.com

Printed in Great Britain
by Amazon

84902319R00108